The Promise of Surfing Rainbows Storybook

This book is
dedicated to
YOU
and all that is
special within
you.

P.D.M Dolce

The Promise of Surfing Rainbows
Written by P.D.M Dolce
With illustrations by Dan Goodfellow
www.dangoodfellow.co.uk
Published by Sentir Ltd.

Please visit our interactive website at www.SurfingRainbows.com for more information
on other great Rainbow Surfing ideas, events, contact information and more.

A special thanks to our friend Sue Roberts for her inspired ideas in the creation
of this book for you

Balboa Press books may be ordered through booksellers or by contacting:

Balboa Press
A Division of Hay House
1663 Liberty Drive
Bloomington, IN 47403
www.balboapress.com
1 (877) 407-4847

ISBN: 978-1-5043-4984-0 (sc)
ISBN: 978-1-5043-4985-7 (e)

Library of Congress Control Number: 2016902363

Print information available on the last page.

Balboa Press rev. date: 03/04/2016

BALBOA
PRESS

A DIVISION OF HAY HOUSE

Introduction

"That must be it!" gasped John, his heart pounding.

"There's no way we can go in there!" exclaimed Maggie, staring straight ahead.

"'Course we can! Come on!" John replied as he raised the collar on his jacket to shield himself from the biting cold wind. They had used up their every last penny on the six hour bus ride to get this far and he was not about to give up now.

Wasting no time, he confidently stepped closer, pulling his sister firmly by the arm. It was their first time in the country, far away from the big city where they lived. They were searching for a new beginning and they were hopeful that they were about to find it.

Although the air was crisp, the sun was shining in the cloudless sky. Everything seemed brighter and cleaner in the country, so different from the dark, dingy street in the city where they lived with their parents.

That morning they had woken up in the pitch-black darkness to catch the 5 o'clock bus. Their Mum had prepared some tea but they had to share the last piece of toast. It was the end of the week and, as usual, the grocery money had run out.

They had begun this quest because John had been brave enough to contact the world-famous singer called Sophia Rose. They were trying to work out what makes a person successful and able to afford the finer things in life. So Maggie had dared John to contact the legendary performer, which was an easy task for him as he was always ready for an adventure.

John knew that Sophia Rose had come from a background similar to theirs. He reckoned that there was always the possibility that she might be prepared to help them and so they sent her a letter. Their friends were astounded that they had been in touch with the famous singer, and even more surprised when she agreed to meet them. Now, here they were, poised to enter her estate, the likes of which they could not have imagined.

"Are we ready for this?" John asked, looking at his sister. They both felt panicky as they approached the large gates to the impressive mansion. Maggie shyly pulled her threadbare coat more tightly around her. "It's so big," she whispered back.

John reached up to ring the bell with a trembling hand and had no idea what to expect. Soon afterwards, the automatic gates opened and they walked through. The long, curving driveway that led to the mansion cut through perfectly trimmed lawns. As they arrived at the front door, it was slowly opened by a cheerful old butler dressed in a dark suit.

He smiled widely. "Won't you come in? Sophia Rose is expecting you," and he gestured for them to come forward. The entrance hall was spacious and filled with a gorgeous scent from the display of flowers on an elegant round table.

Maggie and John were shown into the sitting room. They carefully walked over the white carpet to sit on the luxurious leather sofa, looking around at their extravagant surroundings; bronze sculptures, rich, dark wooden furniture and stunning paintings on the walls. It was very different from the tiny flat they shared with their parents.

The friendly butler picked up a tray with cakes, glasses and a jug of homemade lemonade from the sideboard. "We thought you might like a snack after your journey," he said placing it on the table in front of them.

"Oh yes!" said John in delight as Maggie murmured a shy, "Thank you very much."

A few moments later a graceful lady in her mid forties, wearing stylish casual clothes came into the room to greet them. Maggie and John jumped up, mouths full of cake, suddenly unsure how to greet their hostess. This was someone who had performed for tens of thousands of people in arenas and theaters all over the world. Maggie felt her heart sink. How on earth could she think that such a person could possibly understand their problems? And more importantly, how on earth could she help them?

Sophia Rose walked over and shook John's hand and then gave Maggie a warm embrace, immediately banishing their fears and the feeling of distance between them. She seemed to speak the same language as they did and something in her sparkling eyes told them that she knew and understood their lives.

Maggie thought Sophia Rose was beautiful, with her long, curly brown hair and deep green eyes. However, it had not been her looks that had made her an international superstar. Everyone who saw her live in concert described how the most remarkable thing about her was not her looks, nor the voice that soared effortlessly through several octaves. No, it was the manner in which she seemed to step out of the way and let the music come through her. Everyone who heard her sing felt as though she was singing directly to them.

Sophia Rose sat down on a comfy chair and was immediately joined by a ginger tomcat who curled up on her lap. "Please do sit down, I can see that you're enjoying your snack," she said with a gentle smile.

They chatted about the bus trip for a while as John reached for another cake. Maggie was terrified to ask the question they had come so far to ask, but as the clock on the wall chimed the hour John blurted out, "You started out poor like us. We don't have a great talent like you do but we're hoping that there must be a way for us to have a better life. We were wondering if you had any tips that could help us. How did you become so successful?"

"Ah! Well I found out about something quite amazing and from then on I always seemed to be in the right place at the right time."

"Wow! What was it? What did you find out?" asked John eagerly.

"Hmm, something very special; something that I still use now," replied Sophia Rose gazing out of the window for a moment.

Maggie was beginning to feel anxious. She wanted to hurry things up. After all, they had come such a long way to ask her advice. The air was full of suspense but both Maggie and John decided to sit quietly and wait.

Turning back to her guests after what seemed like ages, Sophia Rose said with great enthusiasm in her voice, "I've been surfing rainbows!"

"Really?!" John replied incredulously, with cake crumbs falling out of his mouth.

Maggie looked at her brother sharply as he dusted the crumbs off his legs and onto the white carpet, then she turned back and said, "What do you mean, 'surfing rainbows'?"

The famous singer chuckled. "Surfing Rainbows is a way of attracting the very best that life has to offer; it makes everything you do become fun and successful!"

Seeing Maggie and John's mix of excitement and confusion, she smiled and decided to share a bit of her life story with them. "As a young girl, I lived in a poor neighborhood, like yours. I always dreamed of becoming a singer and touring the world, but I didn't dare tell many people because I was scrawny and not particularly pretty. I had asthma and sometimes my breathing was difficult; not exactly a promising start for a great singing career!"

"Whenever I did share my ideas with anyone, they just laughed at me, saying that it was an impossible dream. But I didn't let that stop me!"

Undeterred by what others thought, Sophia Rose would practice breathing and singing every day as she walked the streets with her little dog, Tilly. "She would wag her tail every time I sang," she said, recounting how she felt that Tilly was the only being on the planet who seemed to believe in her.

One day Sophia Rose and Tilly were in the local run-down park. As always, she was singing. Her eyes were shut, and she was enjoying great comfort in her song. To her surprise she heard someone behind her say, "You have a wonderful voice!"

"My eyes flew open wide and I spun around to see the local high school music teacher standing in front of me. I'll never forget the look on her face! She paid me another compliment and then said that she would be happy to give me some free, private singing lessons."

Sophia Rose looked deep into John and Maggie's eyes as she continued her story. At her first singing lesson, the woman did something that was to change her life. The teacher gave her a book, a very special book called *The Promise of Surfing Rainbows*. At first, Sophia Rose thought the book was just about some enchanted creatures, but she soon grasped that it was actually packed full of very useful ancient wisdom.

"As soon as I started using it, things always seemed to work out well for me," she said.

Maggie and John were both listening intently to Sophia Rose's story but they were totally unprepared for what she said next.

"Anyone can do it," she exclaimed. "Anyone can go surfing rainbows! It doesn't matter what your background is, and it doesn't matter what you want, because surfing rainbows can help you achieve anything!"

Sophia Rose explained how she still read a few of the cherished pages every day, and although she had shared the information with her own children, she had been waiting for the right time to pass on the book to someone outside of her own family, just as it had been passed on to her.

"And, I think that this is the moment I've been waiting for."

Astounded, Maggie and John raised their eyebrows as they heard their invitation to go into the study to read her most prized possession, the book that the music teacher had given to her all those years ago.

Preparing to stand, Sophia Rose slowly stroked the cat on her lap, nudging it softly to wake it up. The cat stretched, opened an eye and was about to make himself comfortable again when she scooped him up, turned and placed him gently on the chair where she had been sitting. She smiled at her visitors and said, "Please, come with me!"

Maggie beamed with joy as she held her breath in excitement. John was sitting on the edge of his chair; his mind was racing. He felt like time had fast-forwarded to his birthday and his favourite uncle was presenting him with the best present ever.

Maggie tugged on his sleeve to get his attention. He turned to her as she stared back at him with questioning eyes, wondering what would happen next. He shrugged his shoulders. He did not have the answer, but they were about to find out.

Sophia Rose stepped forward towards the two large wooden doors that opened into the next room. The guests quickly glanced at each other and then scanned the large room ahead. The study was vast and full of leather bound books that neatly lined the polished shelving. Sophia Rose stepped to the side and said, "I wonder if you realize how significant this moment is both for you and for me..."

Speechless, they looked up at her, again not sure what to say. She held out her hand and beckoned them to come forward.

In the middle of the huge bookcase they saw a glass cabinet, and behind the glass was what they were looking for, the book called *The Promise of Surfing Rainbows*. They stared at it without moving.

The children heard the large doors close quietly behind them. They were on their own now. If they read this book, would they also have a successful life like Sophia Rose? If they were half as successful as she had been, they would be doing very well!

They never noticed how well worn the handle of the cabinet was because they were too absorbed with its contents. John boldly strode forward to open the cabinet. He hesitated, then he leaned in and gently grasped the book with both hands.

He took his time as he ran his fingers over the glossy, colourful cover, feeling the frayed edges of the soft spine.

"What are you waiting for? Let me see it!" Maggie's eyes were full of hope as she reached out to him.

He turned to her and asked, "What do you think it's about?"

"Open it and see!" said Maggie as she gestured impatiently for him to sit on the couch by the window, so they could read it together.

As they sat down, they glanced out of the window and noticed that it had started raining. Through the droplets, the sun was still shining and a beautiful rainbow appeared in front of them.

"What a coincidence!" said John quietly as he slowly and respectfully opened the cover of the book, eager to find the treasure within the words on its pages.

The Awakening

There have always been rainbows that appear in the sky; beautiful, coloured arcs of light that form when the sunshine hits drops of water as the rain falls.

There are other rainbows too, very special rainbows, which are the home of some fascinating creatures, each of whom bears the colour of its part of the rainbow. These Rainbow Surfers, as they are called, will slide down their rainbow to set out on a journey into that part of the world we cannot see, hear or touch in the usual way. Yet, we know this world exists, because these Rainbow Surfers live in each of us.

Now it is the time of their awakening.

The Rainbow Surfers had been snoozing for what seemed like a lifetime. Pearl the Hawk woke first and looked around at her friends sleeping close by as they floated, each in his or her part of the rainbow, with their colours shining through the darkness.

Pearl always trusted that everything would go well, so she was looking forward to enjoying every bit of the journey. She looked fondly at each of her friends in turn, knowing some of them might find the trip quite challenging.

Clay the Badger was sleeping where the rainbow touched the ground. She was a gentle creature who was often rooted to the spot because she was not keen on change, even when there was something much better just around the corner.

Sunny the Giraffe slept standing up with his head in the clouds. He tended to plod through life aimlessly. At times he seemed sad and disappointed because he was still searching for something to give his life more meaning and fun.

Booster the Lion was stretched out along his part of the rainbow, snoring loudly. His beautiful mane, which he always thought looked messy, fell across his eyes. Although Booster appeared strong, he did not always feel very good about himself.

Minty the Crocodile seemed to be paddling along as he slept. While he looked a little scary, he had a heart full of love that he longed to share. Although he could be snappy, most of the time his big heart showed through and he was as soft as putty.

Chatty the Frog was only half asleep because she was troubled by some worries that she was keeping to herself. She usually had a lot to say but not lately. Pearl the Hawk knew that Chatty the Frog would have to rise above her problems to be able to enjoy the trip.

Iris the Butterfly was resting almost at the top of her part of the rainbow. As she always followed her inspiration, her mind was trouble free and she slept well, with her beautiful deep blue and lavender-coloured wings folded gently over her back.

When dawn arrived and the world grew light, Booster the Lion called out, "Let's go and explore!" Watching his friends prepare for the trip, he looked curiously at Chatty the Frog, who was busily filling bags of all different shapes and sizes.

"What are you doing?" asked Booster the Lion.

"Er, packing. Aren't you taking anything?" replied Chatty the Frog, realizing for the first time that the others had no bags with them.

Sunny the Giraffe smiled cheekily, slowly blinking his big brown eyes at her. "Do you really need all that old stuff?" he asked.

"Yes! Be ready for the worst, I always say!" replied Chatty. She stopped and thought about it for a moment and then looked bothered as she wondered whether it might be time to leave her old things behind. She put her bags down carefully, then picked them all up, only to hesitate a few moments later and drop them down beside her webbed feet again.

Out of the corner of her eye, Chatty the Frog noticed that Clay the Badger was peering out at the world below through the opening in their special rainbow.

Clay the Badger moved forward and then backed away, scared of stepping out. Booster the Lion waved his paws in front of Clay's dazed eyes and whispered, "We won't go without you. Come to the edge!"

"Ooh I'm not sure," said Clay, trembling with fright.

"Come to the edge," encouraged Booster kindly.

"Ooh!" was Clay the Badger's response as she took a step closer.

"Come to the edge!" demanded Booster the Lion somewhat impatiently. He was about to walk behind and push her out when she took a deep breath and jumped forward. Chatty the Frog gasped in surprise as she watched her friend and it gave her the confidence to take a big step of her own. She decided it was time to leave her old baggage behind.

When Clay the Badger had gingerly leapt forward through the opening in their special rainbow, she was followed by Sunny the Giraffe, Booster the Lion, Minty the Crocodile, Chatty the Frog and Iris the Butterfly. Pearl the Hawk gracefully flew out to join her friends as well.

And so the Rainbow Surfers began their amazing journey.

They felt like the first pioneers discovering a new world. It used to be said that the world was flat, now they knew it was round. But perhaps the Rainbow Surfers would find out that the world was multi-faceted like a perfectly cut jewel, or perhaps even multi-dimensional. It was Pearl the Hawk who knew that the world they were about to discover would actually be a reflection of their own hopes, fears and desires.

Having passed through the opening, they clambered up the outside of their rainbow until they reached the top of the slippery arch. They laughed as they slid down the other side. Picking up speed, their excitement increased and the wind whizzed past like a fantastic burst of freedom. As they surfed the curves of the smooth, steep rainbow slide they were amazed when they saw what was ahead.

The Lands of Potential and Possibilities

Minty the Crocodile dived, somersaulted, regained his balance and raced in front of the others. He was scooting along on his back paws, surfing the rainbow like an expert. Then he lifted one foot in the air and sped mono-ski down the green run. He cheered and laughed with joy.

The group of friends ended up in a heap at the foot of their rainbow, a bed of feathers cushioning their arrival. When they rose to their feet, they brushed away the clinging feathers and looked around to find that they were standing on a large terrace. Scattered all around them were large golden coins glistening in the sunlight. Amongst the treasure Booster the Lion noticed one particularly shiny coin with some words on it. They all gathered around to take a closer look.

Iris the Butterfly was thrilled because she knew its significance, "We're going to need this coin later. Let's take it with us!" she said.

Booster the Lion gladly picked it up. As he was about to put it in his pocket for safe-keeping, he noticed that there were some words on the flipside of it as well, although that side of the coin was a murky brown colour rather than the shiny bright gold. He wanted to take a few more gold coins but he was not sure if he should, so he left the rest behind.

They had arrived in the middle of a carnival at a place called The Here and Now. The carnival grounds were set on a hillside within parkland surrounded by large old cypress trees. The terrace where they stood was in the cool shade and beneath them were some beautiful gardens which sloped gently down to a sandy bay and the clear warm waters of a large river.

The friends were keen to take a closer look at what was going on at the carnival. They could see all sorts of cars in a parade along the river's edge. It was a wonderful mix of vintage, modern and futuristic vehicles. The drivers were all wearing funny hats and colourful clothes. There was a band playing and plenty of onlookers were having fun as they waved at the passing drivers.

From their position on the terrace the Rainbow Surfers could look beyond the carnival and admire the spectacular far-reaching views of the Lands of Potential and Possibilities.

While the group of friends chatted, Pearl the Hawk flew a little closer to the river and perched on the roots of an old oak tree. She beckoned to the others to join her, "I've some fantastic news about our trip. Come over here and I'll tell you!"

The Navigator

Pearl always seemed to know what path to follow and now she took on the role of leader. She waited for her friends to rush over and gather around her before she exclaimed dramatically, "Welcome to the River of Life!"

Before anyone could say anything, she pointed towards the water with the tip of her wing and continued, "...and there are your LightShips!" As expected, the Rainbow Surfers' reactions varied, ranging from Clay the Badger's concern to Minty the Crocodile's curiosity.

Chatty the Frog stared at the magnificent ships and asked, "Where shall we go in them?"

"Anywhere! You can go anywhere you like once you know how to sail them," explained Pearl the Hawk. "There are some wonderful places to visit, like The Krystal Kavern."

The group fell silent at the mention of The Krystal Kavern. Then, Clay the Badger spoke up. "I've heard a lot about it, but I don't know anyone who's actually been there."

"Ah," said Pearl, "It's an amazing place, more beautiful and more wonderful than you can imagine."

"In what way?" asked Booster the Lion.

"It's hard to describe. You'll have to discover that for yourself."

"Let's get our LightShips to take us there! Let's go there now!" said Booster eagerly.

"Great idea, but how do we sail them?" asked Minty the Crocodile.

"You know that gold coin you found amongst the treasure at the end of our rainbow? The instructions for our LightShips are on that," Pearl said, turning to Booster the Lion who immediately took the coin out of his pocket and gave it to her.

The friends looked at each other in wonder as Pearl the Hawk studied the words then she looked up at her good friends, smiled and said, **"Your LightShip automatically heads towards what you want when you think thoughts that make you feel good but it turns and heads the other way when you think thoughts that make you feel bad."**

Sunny the Giraffe frowned as he said in a grumpy voice, "No good for me then, I feel bad quite often."

Pearl continued to say, "Don't worry. You have a Navigator, if you get sidetracked and head off in the wrong direction, then your Navigator will let you know how to get back on course!"

"I'd like to meet this Navigator," said Sunny the Giraffe.

Pearl paused for a second or two and then said, "You can't see or meet the Navigator, but you can't see the wind, nor touch shadows…even though you know they're there!"

The group of friends turned to gaze at the LightShips. Clay the Badger was biting her claws as she gave the others a quick glance before turning back to stare blankly at Pearl the Hawk. She was not at all convinced. She could not see how her LightShip would automatically go in this or that direction, and she was even more concerned about receiving guidance from an invisible Navigator.

Pearl smiled reassuringly and said, **"Everyone has a Navigator. That includes YOU…yes YOU…Your Navigator's guidance is very clear. You receive it through your feelings."**

"Really?" asked Chatty the Frog.

"Your Navigator can guide you to BE whatever, DO whatever, and GO wherever you want along the River of Life, whether you're on land or in your LightShips!"

Booster the Lion looked stunned. "Are you sure?" he asked.

"Oh yes!" chirped back Pearl the Hawk. **"Your Navigator can guide you ANYWHERE to enjoy ANY type of experience."**

Booster rubbed his chin and growled, "*ANYWHERE? ANY* type of experience?"

"Absolutely!" replied Pearl boldly.

"Wow!" muttered Sunny the Giraffe.

The Rainbow Surfers were excited because it is one thing to have a dream. It is quite another to actually have the power to make it come true! Their heads were spinning at the thought.

Clay the Badger leaned forward and rested her elbows on her knees as she fixed her gaze on Pearl. Chatty the Frog screwed up her face in concentration and the other Rainbow Surfers also leaned in closer as Pearl the Hawk continued to chat away.

"When you begin to feel low, that's your Navigator's way of guiding you to change the thoughts that are upsetting you, to find something that makes you feel a little better and a bit more hopeful.

As you start paying attention to the things that make you feel good, your LightShip will also change direction and get back on track and start heading towards your dreams and desires again.

Basically when you feel good, you are following your Navigator's advice and you are going in the right direction, but when you're feeling bad you're going in the wrong direction.

It's so simple really!" Pearl cooed.

She clapped her wings together and said, "If you stumbled across a genie in a bottle, you'd be offered three wishes but your Navigator gives you as many wishes as you want. So you'll always, always, ALWAYS be able to achieve ALL your dreams and ALL your desires!"

The rest of the Rainbow Surfers looked back at her in awe. All except Clay the Badger who still wasn't clear on how she was going to sail her LightShip. Nor did she really understand how she would know which direction she should be sailing in. She sat there quietly feeling very unsure but not wanting to ask any questions. Pearl the Hawk could sense Clay's unease but knew that one way or another she would soon get the hang of what to do.

The rest of the group was raring to go, and they quickly made their way down the hill to the jetty on the River of Life where the gleaming LightShips were moored. Ripples in the warm, blue water were winding downstream. It was a glorious, hot, sunny day and it seemed to be snowing white blossoms, while a gentle breeze was bursting with the scent of flowers.

The Rainbow Surfers had been intrigued by what their friend Pearl had told them and they were mesmerized by what they saw on the water.

CHAPTER

Passing The NotSoSure Shop

Minty the Crocodile was speechless as he approached the jetty. He stopped in his tracks and pointed towards the sparkling LightShips. When the others followed his stare, they were also fascinated by what they saw. The LightShips were right in front of them, but they were shimmering in a bright light, as though they were an illusion.

"Are they real?" asked Chatty the Frog twitching her nose anxiously.

"Yes, yes of course they are!" roared Booster the Lion while blinking a few times and shaking his head as if to wake himself up.

Most of the friends were in a hurry to reach their ships and didn't even notice The NotSoSure Shop that had caught Clay the Badger's eye on the way. Although Clay definitely wanted to go on their adventure, the idea of having to steer her own LightShip with how she felt made her very nervous. What if she sank it? What if she drowned? She looked up at the sign for The NotSoSure Shop and ducked inside. Maybe her friends would not notice that she was missing if she just stayed indoors until they left.

Inside she found many helpful assistants who had plenty of warnings about what to watch out for on the trip along the river. Listening to their dreadful warnings really made Clay think that going on the river was not a good idea. Oh yes, it was much safer to stay on dry land!

As she glanced out the window, she noticed that Minty the Crocodile was about to turn around to check if she was all right. Not wanting to draw attention to herself, she popped out onto the doorstep to wave and smile at him. He returned the smile, waved and stepped on board his LightShip. Clay then quickly stepped back inside the shop.

Meanwhile, the rest of the Rainbow Surfers had discovered old wooden chests full of gadgets at the helm of their LightShips. Booster the Lion was the first to open his and find a paint ball gun. His friends were quick to do the same!

Roaring with laughter, a paint ball fight soon started. Slipping and sliding on the decks of their ships, they darted about whilst aiming paint balls at each other. A splat of yellow paint from Booster the Lion just missed Minty the Crocodile's ear but Sunny the Giraffe's squirt of sticky orange was a direct hit and took him by surprise.

Chatty the Frog skillfully hopped out of the way of a few shots and then fired a few scorchers of her own, to her friends' surprise. They chuckled, snorted and laughed out loud as they skidded about, covered in splats of different coloured paint, which trickled down toward their feet.

Clay the Badger looked out of the window again to see the fun her friends were having, but it made no difference. She was always afraid of trying anything new.

As the friends recovered from their paint ball battle, still chuckling and firing a few shots in the air, Minty the Crocodile turned to ask, "Where's Clay?" Remembering that he had last waved to her at The NotSoSure Shop, he put down his gun and walked up the river bank towards the shop.

As he reached the entrance, he hastily tried to rub off the worst of the paint splatters but only succeeded in smudging them even more. Minty looked such a mess the shop assistants just shook their heads and wouldn't let him go in!

Just then Clay the Badger looked out of the window again and Minty's face broke into a big smile.

"Clay! What are you doing here? Come and join us!"

Clay winced fearfully.

"I'm not sure that the Navigator will help me." she murmured.

"Of course it will help you! You'll be fine," said Minty. "You'll have fun. Come on, let's go!"

After a few moments, Clay appeared at the door of the shop. She was walking very oddly and Minty looked at her in alarm. On her feet were a savage looking pair of boots with large spiky soles.

"What are you wearing those for?" he asked.

"The shop assistants said I would need something to help me stay upright on the deck of my ship," replied Clay, looking uneasy as she hobbled towards the river with her friend.

"Oh that's crazy! You'd pierce a hole in it the minute you step on board," Minty the Crocodile said laughing. "Let me help you take them off!"

Clay hesitated but looked a little relieved. She hadn't been sure about the advice The NotSoSure Shop's assistants had given her, and the boots really did hurt! She sat down on a nearby log and together they untied the boots. They chatted about other things for a while and Clay began to feel much happier again.

She confidently shook her right leg to rid it of the boot, but it stubbornly remained in place. She struggled to pry it off and then she threw it aside. As she pulled off her second boot, she had the urge to kick it off and she smiled as it landed in The NotSoSure Shop's recycling bin.

When Clay the Badger stood up, happy to be free of her boots, she turned and looked at the river and hesitated. Minty stretched out his paint-covered hand for her to hold and together they walked to the river's edge.

Nervously, Clay inched closer to the beautiful, clear water. As she knelt down to peer in, something dark and stripy quivered on the surface. She let out a cry and quickly backed away, but it had been her own reflection that surprised her! Clay sighed and gave a watery smile.

Clay slowly, very slowly, stepped on board her LightShip. The ship wobbled and her worst fears came true! When the left side of the ship was about to go under, she launched herself to the right side. The ship rocked unsteadily and she hurled herself back to the left side again. She looked as if she was doing a wild tribal dance until finally she fell head over heels into the water.

She didn't know how to swim! Panic stricken, Clay the Badger desperately splashed about, scrambling back up the riverbank as fast as she could.

The Soaked Badger

Two sopping wet ears appeared first.

She pulled with her front paws and pushed with her back ones as she heaved herself up and out, crawling a little way along the riverbank before standing up. A puddle soon formed at her feet. The soaked Badger had soggy-wet, sticking-up fur and big sorry eyes.

The Rainbow Surfers looked at each other in shock, they hadn't understood just how scared Clay had been. Pearl the Hawk flew to her side and said, "With your heavy worries, you were bound to fall in the water. You told yourself you would and you did."

Still dripping, Clay picked the reeds from her fur and wiped herself down with a towel she found by the side of a barrel. She looked pained as she muttered in a hushed, trembling voice, "Oooh, I've never been on a ship before and I didn't think I'd manage to maneuver it. How can I be sure that I'm going to get the Navigator's guidance?" she sighed.

"It's easy. Your Navigator talks to you through your feelings. When you trust its guidance it really will keep you safe and guide you to wherever you want to go on the River of Life," said Pearl the Hawk soothingly. Then she asked, "Can you tell me, using a scale of 0-10, where 0 is terrible and 10 is great, how you're feeling about what's just happened?"

Clay looked uncomfortable as she replied, "Er. Yes…that was a…0…I think."

Pearl smiled triumphantly, moved closer and rested her wing on Clay the Badger's damp shoulder before saying, "That's it! That's all you have to do! **Ask yourself how you feel about something and you'll get the Navigator's answer."**

"What do you mean?" asked Clay looking more baffled than ever.

"OK, so let's go back. How did you feel on a scale of 0-10 about The NotSoSure Shop's advice?"

"Oh, terrible. That was definitely a 0! It didn't seem right at all, but they made themselves out to be the experts, so I thought I had better do what they said."

Pearl nodded. "When you felt bad, that was your Navigator telling you that you were doing something, or were about to do something, that was taking you away from what you wanted."

"Er?" replied Clay.

"You wanted to come on the trip, didn't you?"

"Oh yes!"

"If you had stayed in The NotSoSure Shop and followed their advice, you wouldn't have come."

"That's true. I wouldn't have come."

"Did you feel good about their boots?"

"No, terrible!"

"And that's because the Navigator knew you didn't need them. When you took them off it felt great, didn't it? You see, whenever you feel great that's how you know you are following your Navigator's advice!"

"Ah!" remarked Clay more confidently. She was beginning to understand. She paused and then said, "But hold on. I also felt bad when I stepped on board my LightShip."

"That's because you wanted to come on the trip but you still weren't sure how to sail. If you had understood how to sail first then you would have felt much better before you set off."

Pearl then held out her wing and uncurled her feathers to reveal the treasured shiny golden coin they had found at the end of their rainbow. Clay's eyes sparkled as she took a closer look at the words written on it.

Upside of FEELING GOOD about trusting your feelings:

Trust your feelings to guide you because when you look for ways to make you feel good you will always feel safe. And, when you think about things that feel good, it draws you to the good experiences you want and the desires you dream about! The 0-10 scale is an easy way to check how good you feel about anything. Whenever you have a choice to make and you trust your feelings you will make the best choice every time!

Downside of FEELING BAD about trusting your feelings:

You change your direction and your destination by where you set your point of view. So when you feel bad aim to find ways of feeling better. The better you feel, the faster you go to what you want and the quicker you arrive!

Clay the Badger looked up and said, "Okay, so I should've stayed on land until I felt better about setting off. And, I shouldn't have taken The NotSoSure Shop's assistants' advice because it didn't feel right. That does make sense."

"How do you feel about your LightShip and your Navigator now?"

Clay smiled and said, "Much better. Yes, I feel good. An 8, I think. I reckon I can pick up my Navigator's advice now. It's quite easy really if all I have to do is check how good I feel. Yes, I reckon I could have a go at sailing."

She felt as if a heavy weight had been lifted off her shoulders, so she confidently stepped forward and this time she happily climbed aboard her LightShip.

Minty the Crocodile called over, "Take a look in the old chest there!" Clay checked where Minty was pointing, reached across, opened it and snatched a paint gun. She swiveled around and squirted a dollop of red paint at Sunny the Giraffe's ear – a perfect direct hit! The others laughed and cheered.

Just then a rather scrumptious smell wafted towards them. Booster the Lion's nose twitched and his ears pricked up with interest. "Where's that coming from?" he shouted.

The others stopped messing around and joined Booster the Lion in pointing their noses in the air towards the direction of the mouth-watering whiff. As they licked their lips and imagined how nice it would be to devour the food, their LightShips began to move in the same direction as the smell, which is where they wanted to go! They looked at each other in amazement. The LightShips really were moving all on their own to where they wanted to go! The Rainbow Surfers were intrigued about what treasures they might find and where the tantalizing scent would lead them.

CHAPTER

Flipping The Parrot's Coin

The friends were so determined to find the source of that tantalizing smell that they hardly noticed how quickly and easily their LightShips took them to the next pier. They moored up and walked inland, where tall trees lined pathways dotted with elegant flowers. As the increasingly hungry group headed down the lane in search of the enticing smell, they chatted enthusiastically about the places they wanted to explore.

Iris the Butterfly noticed that Sunny the Giraffe was plodding along slowly behind the others. He had a distant look in his eyes as he wandered along, gazing at nothing in particular. He always avoided disappointment by trying not to think about what he wanted to do, or where he wanted to go, just in case he didn't make it.

Iris the Butterfly fluttered her wings and flew up alongside her friend to interrupt his vacant thoughts, "What are you thinking about?" she asked.

"Nothing, why?" replied Sunny.

"The rest of us are excited but you don't seem to be. What do you want from your trip on the River of Life?"

"I haven't really thought about it. I guess I'd quite like to have my own collection of tasty leaves, but I'm not going to get my hopes up because I'll just feel let down if I don't find them," replied Sunny with a faint smile as he continued to amble slowly down the track.

"Oh yes, do get your hopes up! Do get excited, otherwise your LightShip will just drift aimlessly down the river! If you're excited about your dreams, it means you'll be feeling great and following your Navigator's guidance, so your LightShip will automatically have to take you to them!"

Sunny stopped, turned towards his friend and then said, "Well, I would like to discover a new variety of really tasty leaves." He paused, adding quickly, "but not spicy leaves!" He shivered at the disgusting thought.

"Only think about what you do want, because then you'll feel happy and your LightShip will go in the right direction." said Iris.

Unsure that Sunny the Giraffe had really grasped how important this was, she then said, "If you think about the things you don't want, it makes you feel bad and your LightShip will sail to what you don't want instead!"

Sunny the Giraffe still looked as though he had a bad taste in his mouth.

Cleverly, Iris the Butterfly decided to ask her friend why he wanted his new collection of leaves, and that was when Sunny's eyes lit up. Now he was definitely thinking about what he wanted! As he imagined having a good munch, he whispered, with a wink, "They'll be my favourite food!" He began to drool at the thought.

Sunny stopped walking and carefully rubbed his neck on a high branch to scratch an itch. After stopping for a moment to think, he then went forward quickly to catch up with his other friends, who were making their way down a pathway that was shaded by large trees. It was leading them towards the ever more enticing smell of good food. As Sunny the Giraffe and Iris the Butterfly turned the corner, they saw their friends passing between two large palm trees and a colourful wooden sign for Parrot's Paradise. They were about to enter through the old doors of the café called Rumblin' Tumm.

Parrot's Paradise

All the tables were full, but a couple of friendly Parrots invited the newcomers to sit down and share their table. A waiter smiled at the group of friends and asked what they would like to drink while they decided what to order.

In the background, Robin the light-footed little bird was expertly running up and down the piano keyboard to the delight of the guests enjoying their meals.

Minty the Crocodile was in a playful mood when he said to Sunny the Giraffe, "Oh, leaves for breakfast, lunch, and tea…why don't you try something different for a change! What about a Chinese meal? There's plenty of tasty looking dishes here; there's Shun Fat or Yuu Stin Ki Pu."

"Yes, yes, good idea," replied Sunny the Giraffe, who was not listening. He had begun to feel very impatient about finding his new collection of leaves. That was when he noticed a strange looking plant behind him. After a few moments, when he saw that everyone at his own table was reading the menu, he awkwardly twisted and stretched his neck back to snatch a large mouthful of leaves from the unusual looking plant.

His large brown eyes opened wide in shock. His eyelids remained motionless as he breathed in sharply, realizing that he had grabbed a mouthful of chili-flavoured leaves by mistake. His nostrils trembled and his eyes began to water as he tried to keep his cool while gulping down the last few drops of nectar from his glass. The sweat streamed down his face and he felt as though he needed a fire extinguisher. That vase of flowers in the middle of the table might do. He quickly pulled the carefully arranged flowers out and without looking, he threw them aside.

As Sunny gulped down the vase-water, the flowers landed across the next table. The poor diner with wet flowers on her plate opened her mouth, ready to shout at Sunny, but thought better of it when she saw Booster the Lion staring back at her. She grumbled quietly to herself and picked the soggy stems out of her dessert. The others watched in surprise as Sunny smiled awkwardly to hide his embarrassment, tried to regain his composure and then fumbled to find his menu. Then he looked innocently around as if nothing had happened.

Iris the Butterfly giggled while sipping from a cup of nettle soup. She knew he couldn't have been following his Navigator's advice, but she decided to chat about that with him later. While the friends munched and slurped and chomped on a selection of fruits and veggies, the usual salad leaves for Sunny the Giraffe and bugs for Chatty the Frog, the Parrots told them about a competition that was just about to start. This was to be a contest of "Heads You Win; Tails You Lose" between the Parrots and the Magpies.

"Oooh, that sounds like fun," said Chatty the Frog.

"You're welcome to come and watch if you like," was the reply.

The game involved flipping coins in the air and then calling "heads" or "tails" before the coin landed. The Magpies always came with plenty of new coins in the hope of winning… but they usually lost.

As the friends left the café and followed the Parrots to where the tournament was about to begin, they were overwhelmed by the mass of brightly coloured feathers at the gathering. A cheerful noise came from the crowd as the teams prepared themselves and the coins were chosen. The scene was stunning; a gorgeous combination of birds, beaks, feathers and fields of sweet-smelling roses.

Pretty Polly was an expert coin flipper and she knew it! She stood pompously rearranging her feathers, admiring herself as she arrogantly shouted out her usual phrase, "Who's the fairest of them all? I am! I am!" She stepped forward, announced her arrival and declared that the International Outdoor Coin-Tossing Championship could begin.

While the birds flipped coins, most of the Rainbow Surfers watched the champs like Lily the Parrot rustle a coin from the ground, spin it on her beak and throw it high into the air. An outburst of noise erupted from the crowd as they yelled out their guesses. Clay the Badger sidled up close to the contestants, watching the Parrots' winning strategy. Chatty the Frog hopped up and down with excitement but then stopped, afraid that one of the coins would fall on her head. She stepped back nervously and gasped as a thorn from one of the roses sharply pricked her side.

Booster the Lion paced back and forth, roaring out his guesses. As the games continued, the tension was rising. Even though Sunny the Giraffe had a good view from his great height, his mind wandered, and he lost interest until another shiny coin was thrown up high enough to catch his attention again.

Despite the rowdy activity, Pearl the Hawk was lazing quietly in the bright midday sun close by with Minty the Crocodile. All of a sudden, Pearl stood up and excitedly pecked the sleeping Crocodile on his back, whipping his ears with her wings. Minty nearly jumped out of his skin as Pearl exclaimed urgently "Wake up! Wake up!"

Minty gasped, "Ouch! Why?"

"See that coin they're throwing?" she asked quickly, "Well, it has two sides to it; 'heads' and 'tails.' Whichever side of the coin you look at determines what you see!" Pearl puffed up her feathers, clearly very impressed with her revelation.

"So what?" snapped Minty, irritated by the rude awakening.

Pearl the Hawk continued to say, "It's like anything you wish for."

"How's that?" responded Minty the Crocodile, looking curious.

Pearl the Hawk was quiet for a moment as she looked up at the sky to gather her racing thoughts. She cleared her throat, then she spoke confidently, "You create your own world."

Minty the Crocodile gave Pearl a sideways glance, tilting his head and raising one scaly eyebrow.

Pearl did not respond. She was deep in thought. She turned around and angled her wing to shield her eyes from the sun so that she could watch her new friends tossing coins.

She saw Sunny the Giraffe sauntering over to them. She waited for him to join them and then continued chatting away, "You see, whatever dream you'd like to experience is rather like the Parrot's Coin they're throwing over there," she suggested. "When you look at the image on one side of a coin you cannot see the different image on the other side. In exactly the same way, every dream you wish for has two sides; the upside and the downside!"

At that she took out their treasured golden coin from her feather pocket and copied the Parrots by flipping it up in the air. She caught it and then she flipped it again towards Sunny the Giraffe, who grabbed it.

Pearl the Hawk declared, **"When the Parrots pick up a coin, they automatically pick up both sides of it. Likewise, when you decide you want something new, you automatically pick up the chance of both the upside of feeling good about it, and the downside of feeling bad about it! So you can either be feeling good that what you want is coming to you soon, or you can be feeling bad that it hasn't come yet."**

Sunny the Giraffe looked at the gleaming coin he was holding. He flipped it over and saw that the words on it had changed, but the meaning was still the same.

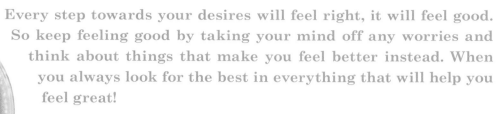

Every step towards your desires will feel right, it will feel good. So keep feeling good by taking your mind off any worries and think about things that make you feel better instead. When you always look for the best in everything that will help you feel great!

Downside of FEELING BAD about the dream you desire:

Flip your feelings from disappointment to cheerful anticipation because when you're feeling down that you don't have what you want yet, that's your problem! That's your problem right there, because as long as you're feeling bad you are moving away from your dreams and desires. You change your direction and your destination by where you set your point of view, so aim to find ways of feeling better. The better you feel, the faster you go towards what you want and the quicker you arrive!

"I thought I had the hang of it," groaned Sunny the Giraffe under his breath. "I was dreaming of having my own collection of new tasty leaves but I ended up with a mouthful of spicy ones instead!"

"You were looking pretty impatient just before you grabbed the spicy leaves," commented Pearl the Hawk, examining Sunny the Giraffe's expression.

"Yes, I suppose I was. Yes, I was feeling very impatient, actually," "And didn't you crook your neck when you grabbed the leaves?" she continued.

"Yup, it still hurts!" he replied, rubbing his sore neck.

"When the Navigator gives you a hunch to do something, you'll feel inspired to do it. It won't feel awkward, and it won't feel like hard work or drudge. It'll make you feel excited and eager to get on and do it; that's how you'll know it's the right thing to do!" said Pearl the Hawk.

It certainly hadn't felt good to Sunny the Giraffe when he had grabbed the spicy leaves. He thought for a moment and then smiled. If looking for ways to feel good lets you know you are on the right path to achieving your desires, that sounded like a plan worth following!

For the first time in a while he was beginning to see clearly through the haze in his mind. He proudly positioned an imaginary LightShip captain's hat on his head. He was determined to be the best captain that he could be and find the tastiest leaves there were to find. He smiled and licked his lips as he pictured himself traveling the world experiencing many new varieties of tasty leaves!

When the coin tossing tournament ended and the Parrots had won yet again, the Rainbow Surfers thanked their hosts and set off back to the jetty where their LightShips were moored.

On the way back, they passed a signpost for The Coral Reef Zone and they decided to take a look. In the warm sun, they walked along a cobbled street that took them down a slope and through an avenue of weeping willows.

On arriving at The Coral Reef Zone, they followed a grassy path that led to a glass platform. At the far corner of the platform stood The Oyster Bar, where Paddy the Oyster was busily adjusting the music coming from the conch seashells. His assistant, Old Joe the Cheery Sole was serving cool nectar drinks and giving out tickets for the show that had already started beneath the glass platform in front of them.

The Rainbow Surfers stepped onto the edge of the platform and watched the brightly coloured fish swimming below. The fish were competing for first place in their fashion show and were parading down the fishwalk, showing off the new season's colours, stripy patterns and scaly textures.

When the show ended, the group of friends made their way back to their LightShips at the jetty, keen to continue their adventures and to find The Krystal Kavern.

Once on board, Sunny the Giraffe's LightShip sailed forward easily as he remembered the words on the golden coin, and was still feeling great about wearing his imaginary Captain's hat and finding his tasty leaves. However some of the other Rainbow Surfers struggled to stay in a straight line in their Lightships, and they kept weaving all over the place from side to side, coming to a halt and stop-starting. When Booster the Lion found himself going round and round in circles, he shouted out, "I've got a duff ship here! What's going on?"

CHAPTER

3

The Magnificent Mane

By trial and error they were beginning to understand the tremendous force behind their thoughts and feelings, because whenever they had any bad thoughts and feelings their LightShips would wander crazily all over the river.

"Ahrrr!" screeched Chatty the Frog, whose eye was beginning to hurt. "Where are we? Why haven't we arrived yet? I bet we're lost! Maybe we're just kidding ourselves. Perhaps this just isn't meant to be!" she groaned, wiping her sore eye.

Pearl the Hawk looked over her shoulder to see Booster's and Chatty's ships rolling around in the water like ping pong balls. She laughed as she called out, **"Whatever you want is whatever is meant to be. That's up to you! Just take your Navigator's advice so that it...can be!"**

Booster the Lion tugged at his mane, as it was getting in his way. He was feeling annoyed and frustrated, "But, it's impossible!" he shouted, "What's the matter with this ship? It won't go where I want!"

"Nothing's the matter. Really, nothing's the matter! That's the whole point! You understood the theory, now put it into practice. Keep going," encouraged Pearl.

"Yes, stop worrying! Remember, you change the direction of your LightShip by how you think and feel! If you're frustrated and angry your LightShip will take you all over the place! So, think about something that makes you feel better, because the better you feel the easier you'll find it on the River of Life!" cried out Iris the Butterfly, whizzing past them all.

Pearl waved at Iris and shouted out "Ha! That's the spirit!"

Booster the Lion's look of surprise soon changed to that of envy, anger and then sheer determination. "If Iris can do it, so can I!" he grumbled to himself under his breath. Iris waved at her friends and called out, **"Remember, the better or worse you feel, the faster your Lightship sails, whether it's to the good experiences you want when you're feeling good, or to the bad experiences you don't want, when you're feeling bad."**

Ignoring Iris's advice, he decided to take action the best way he knew how by roaring, pacing up and down, shoving and blowing on his sails, but his LightShip veered off course even more. Not one to be outdone by a butterfly, Booster the Lion let out another mighty roar, and used all his might to struggle on.

Booster soon grew exhausted, even though he remained determined. The blood vessels on his neck bulged. He felt like a boiling kettle with steam shooting out of his nose and ears. His ship moved faster and faster, but in the wrong direction.

Finally Booster realized that the more he pushed himself, the more annoyed and worn out he felt, and the more his LightShip sailed the wrong way. Iris the Butterfly looked back and called out again, **"You have to change your point of view if you want to change your direction!"**

It was clear to Booster the Lion that he needed a new approach. Could it really be true that the LightShip was picking up his angry thoughts and bad feelings? He flopped back and sat down to think it over and as he began to relax a little, he began to feel better. That was when he felt drawn to look behind him and he saw that the rudder on his LightShip was jammed with reeds. He tugged on the rudder to free it. Once dislodged, his ship was immediately propelled forward in the right direction.

Although pleased, he soon felt embarrassed for not keeping up with the others in the first place. Then he grew even more irritated than before, "How could a butterfly have known better than me? What must the others think of me now?"

Chatty the Frog looked over her shoulder and noticed that Booster was drifting towards the ridge of a dangerous waterfall. She saw his look of frustration turn to panic as he desperately started rushing around again, trying to regain control of his LightShip by whacking and pouncing on its sails just as he had before.

"What's happening!" gasped Booster. "Nooooo!" he roared as the turbulent whirlpools at the edge of the waterfall appeared rapidly in front of him.

His efforts were futile.

Panting, the terrified lion looked ahead and gulped. He felt confused, breathless and dizzy.

The spinning whirlpools seemed to be drifting closer and closer. He had one ear raised and the other half folded. Just then his mind filled with doubts as he wondered how his panicky thoughts could be sending him off course now. He also wondered how he was supposed to calm his mind when he was heading right for the waterfall! But it was coming closer and he needed his LightShip to change direction. So finally he decided that he had better try what Iris had said.

He covered his eyes with his soft paws and concentrated hard, trying to pull his attention away from the chaos surrounding him.

The Rescue

Once he felt calmer, he removed his paws from his eyes, but his thumping headache soon returned when he saw the edge of the waterfall looming ever closer. It was all happening so fast that it was difficult to still his racing thoughts. The waves crashed against his ship and the water splashed in his face, as if demanding he take note of what he had to do.

He bravely concentrated all his will power again, and surprised even himself. "Come on now, think of something good! Think of something good! Well right now **WHAT DO I WANT?** …I want to be on the riverbank and I want to find The Krystal Kavern…"

He took some deep breaths and tried to calm his mind again. He imagined himself being safely up by the riverbank and then exploring The Krystal Kavern, and that felt good! It felt very good! Then he asked himself…**WHY DO I WANT THAT?**

He kept thinking about all sorts of different reasons why he wanted to be up by the riverbank, like being safe and having fun with his friends.

He did manage to change his point of view and that made him feel much better.

Booster continued to imagine being up by the riverbank and at The Krystal Kavern until his mood had definitely shifted from fear to feeling genuinely excited. **And as soon as he changed his point of view, his thoughts immediately changed his feelings and the direction of his LightShip.**

Unknown to the group of friends, Thomas the Pelican had flown past and overheard the commotion below. He alerted James the Monkey, who slid down and swung between the branches of the bendy trees overhanging the river, as if he were riding a big dipper at an amusement park. In no time at all, he landed right in front of his friend Edward the Elephant. James scrambled swiftly up Edward's trunk shouting in his enormous ears that they had some rescuing to do.

A few heartbeats later, the Elephant's large grey figure emerged from the shadows. Convinced that they should help, he blew his trumpet to sound a loud alert. He waded into the water with James the Monkey perched on top of his head, tightly gripping onto his big ears. He saw a tree stump sticking up that marked the way to a channel of calmer waters and a little pier at the river's edge.

Edward the Elephant called out, "Look over here! Come to this side of the stump!" whilst James the Monkey signaled madly, as if directing traffic.

Booster the Lion spotted Edward, James and the stump and let out a huge sigh of relief. Moments later, his LightShip bumped haphazardly into some rocks and spun around. As if by chance, his ship was tossed over towards the safer, quieter waters to the left of the tree stump. All it took was a few seconds.

The other Rainbow Surfers were watching with bated breath.

"Phew! Thank goodness for that!" uttered Chatty the Frog, wiping her brow.

"Oh Booster was so lucky that the Monkey and Elephant were around to help!" exclaimed Clay the Badger.

"That wasn't luck," replied Iris the Butterfly.

"What do you mean?" asked Minty the Crocodile, frowning.

"The Navigator works in amazing ways," remarked Iris the Butterfly with a knowing smile.

"What?" cried Minty, with his big jaw open in disbelief.

"It may seem like luck when you follow your Navigator's guidance, but somehow it always helps you solve your problems," explained Iris.

Well, whatever had just happened, Booster did feel very lucky indeed. He smiled gratefully and gave a nod of thanks to his new friends.

Later, when they all set off in their LightShips Booster felt victorious as he took the lead. The Rainbow Surfers were all proud of themselves. The idea of steering their ships with their thoughts and feelings was still very new to them, but they were managing quite well now and there was less of the crazy weaving to and fro and more of a calm and steady course. They carried on looking for things to feel good about and felt triumphant when they saw a jetty in the distance.

A Pit Stop

"Oh!" said Booster the Lion as they approached the dock. He turned to Pearl the Hawk and moaned, "Look!"

He was pointing up at the sign above them, which was dazzling in the sunshine. It read, "Welcome to The FabFunFairground."

Pearl merely said, "So?"

"But I want to go to The Krystal Kavern!" groaned Booster.

"Me too!" added Chatty the Frog rubbing her left eye, which was still hurting her. "Maybe we'll never find it. Maybe we're just fooling ourselves!" she moaned.

"If you keep going in the right direction, you'll eventually arrive at your destination, whatever and wherever that is! If it feels good to stop here, then that's our Navigator nudging us for a reason," came back the reply.

"I'd like to stay here for a few days; it feels very good to me!" piped up Clay the Badger, glancing at a long list of rides they could go on. "And look! They have a Spa here, too. I'll have a soak in the hot tub at The Soap Opera." She beamed a wicked grin at Sunny the Giraffe and said, "You could have a nice, long neck massage."

The Rainbow Surfers had a few turns on some of the most incredibly-wacky looking FabFunFairground rides before reaching the Spa center. They felt ready for a little break from their journey. Eva the Koala met them when they entered through some large, wooden doors and showed them to a quiet, relaxing room.

As they walked down a long corridor, the Rainbow Surfers couldn't help but notice the strange looking plants that lined the walls. These were obviously Eva the Koala's greatest pride and joy.

Chatty the Frog kept her eyes glued on Booster the Lion's swishing tail. Moments later she was skidding along the floor, lunging after a fragile plant pot that Booster's tail had sent flying. With her naturally-shaped baseball-gloved hands outstretched, her body hit against the wall of the corridor and slid down. She reached out the tip of her mitt a little further and a little further still until she caught the flying missile. It slipped out of her grasp, but she caught it again to the spontaneous cheer from the imaginary crowd in her head.

She stood up, replaced the pot, and quickly snatched Booster's tail, keeping it firmly and gently under control as if it were a wedding-train, until they reached the room where Eva the Koala invited the friends to enjoy the relaxing spa treatments on offer.

Booster sighed heavily when Chatty the Frog let go of his tail. He looked for a seat in the far corner of the large room. On sitting down he caught a glimpse of his reflection in the big mirrors on the walls. Clay the Badger noticed him looking down at the floor, shuffling his paws awkwardly.

Sensing that he was being watched, Booster looked up to see his friend kindly smiling back at him. "What's up?" she asked.

"I'm fine," Booster answered. He looked around at the others, trying to think of something to say that would hide his bad mood.

Clay the Badger looked at him, puzzled, and then said, "What's wrong? I can tell something's wrong."

Booster the Lion sighed, "I don't feel so good about myself."

Clay the Badger turned around and strode purposefully over to Sunny the Giraffe who was in the middle of being given a deep neck massage. She tapped him on the shoulder and, as Sunny knew what she wanted, he moved himself around a little and reached inside his pocket. He pulled out their shiny, treasured golden coin and gave it to her. Clay took it over to Booster the Lion and placed it carefully in his big paw.

Upside of FEELING GOOD about yourself: You are magnificent!

How good you feel about yourself is up to you! You're unique and amazing just the way you are! You're fabulous in your own wonderful way! There has never been anyone like you! What you believe is up to you. So, believe it. It's true!

Think about the things you do like about yourself. When you genuinely feel better about yourself, you shift into a better mood and that draws you to the good experiences you want and the desires you dream about!

Downside of FEELING BAD about yourself:

When you feel bad about anything, including yourself, you move away from the dreams you want. You change your direction and your destination by where you set your point of view, so aim to find ways of feeling better. The better you feel, the faster you go towards what you want and the quicker you arrive!

He stroked his mane, which he had thought was a big, bushy mess. How could he feel better about it? He decided to do what the coin said and think about the bits of himself that he did like until he began to feel a little better. In fact, he did think his big powerful paws were very impressive, and his sparkly eyes were rather dashing too. He continued until he did indeed feel much better about himself and soon his messy mane did not seem so important. The wrinkled lines on his forehead relaxed. Maybe he'd look strange without his mane! Maybe it was magnificent and not so messy after all!

Booster kept thinking about his mane while his friends were enjoying the treatments at the Spa. Finally his thoughts were interrupted as he heard some sounds of laughter and funky music outside.

"Ooh what's going on out there?" asked Minty the Crocodile as he cocked his head to listen.

The group was intrigued. They thanked Eva the Koala for looking after them so well and then they went outside. They all gathered around Sunny the Giraffe, who had the best view, thanks to his height. He turned to where the music was coming from. "It looks like a party," he grinned. "Let's go and find out!"

They made their way back to the jetty, making a detour past the The FabFunFairground again, so that they could have another turn on some of the best FabFunRides. Booster the Lion was feeling so much happier about himself as he flew down the rollercoaster with his mane blowing in the wind. By the time he stepped on board his Lightship he was beginning to feel that it was definitely a magnificent mane after all!

Earthrocks at Boogie Garden

Soon they were all sailing in their LightShips towards Earthrocks at The Boogie Garden, where the cool music was oozing out of the stones. A light, refreshing breeze welcomed them as they arrived at the next jetty. The trees moved to the music in a sway-funky-dance and the plants twirled around, clicking their petals. A few crickets joined in to the bluesyjazz tunes and the youngest members of their group improvised when the cool moves were just a little too tricky for their little legs.

A grumpy centipede, who was balancing on a rocking leaf, refused to join in, but everyone else at The Boogie Garden seemed to be having fun.

Even the blades of grass were doing the twist. Overhead a passing flock of birds made a screeching noise in unison as they slammed on their brakes with both feet, coming to a halt in midair, repositioning themselves, and then boogieing to the catchy rhythm. After a good workout, they continued on their way with their snooty beaks pointing up high as they majestically flew off in proper formation in the clear, crisp sky.

Pearl was perched on a branch behind the others, where she could see the various sizes and shapes of her friends' tails wagging in time to the music. She called down to them, saying that she had a game for them to play. They were to line up and put on some blindfolds. There was quite a distance between each contestant and a big open space in front of them. When the starter whistle was blown, they had to run straight ahead for 200 meters down a slope, go round a ditch and then continue until they crossed a gravel path, which was the finish line at the end of the track.

As Minty the Crocodile set off, he waddled left a bit, then right a bit, trying to peep through his blindfold. He sprinted forward, then he swerved sharply off to the left.

"Oh, this is easy!" cried Sunny the Giraffe, who promptly smacked his head on a swinging branch that sent him off to the right. He plodded on, but the route he had taken by mistake sent him towards some thorny bushes. He scraped himself as he trudged knee-high into a swamp, and then he was totally confused about which way to turn next.

Sunlight flickered through the branches and the willowy trees were still sway-funky-dancing to the rhythm from the rocks and rustling the leaves on their lower branches like cheerleaders' pom-poms. Now and again a thud thud thud noise could be heard in the background when a magnificent old oak tree joined in by tapping his roots on the sun-baked ground, keeping the beat as if playing the drums.

Meanwhile, Booster the Lion had been very carefully pacing the steps ahead of him and although he had gone forward in a very crooked line, he still managed to reach the gravel path first. He purred as he pushed up his blindfold. His contented purring noise grew louder and louder. He sat down with a beaming smile on his face, looking back at the others.

The rest of the group zigzagged off, scrambling in all directions, stumbling over each other and finally crashing into a huge pile. Some of them took off their blindfolds as they tumbled around laughing and slapping each other on the back.

Other animals gathered around, balancing on the swaying branches or the shaking ground as they cheered the Rainbow Surfers on from the sideline, clapping their paws and hooves.

When the laughter had died down and they had all removed their blindfolds, Pearl the Hawk pointed out that if they did not set their sights clearly on where they wanted to go, they would end up all over the place. She explained that it's the same on the River of Life. They needed to set their sights clearly on their dreams and desires, and then follow their Navigator's guidance to take them there.

Grinning cheekily, Booster the Lion turned to his friend and asked, "Well the dream I desire is to be rich! Can the Navigator help me with that too?"

"Absolutely!" was Pearl the Hawk's response. "It can help you with anything!"

"Don't you have to work extremely hard and be very old to become rich?" asked Clay the Badger.

"If that's what you believe, then that'll be true for you, but it doesn't have to be that way. You can believe what you want. When you believe that you can be happy, healthy and wealthy all at the same time, then you can be! Dream yourself enjoying whatever experience you want to enjoy and then your Navigator really will help take you there."

Sunny the Giraffe nodded as he took a moment to enjoy dreaming about himself discovering his delicious new leaves. A little while later he heard someone sneeze behind him. As he turned around and looked down, he saw a pack of wolf cubs looking back up at him. One of them asked if they could join in the next game.

Other new contestants also met up with the Rainbow Surfers as they strolled over to a different racetrack, which started out in a field and finished behind some sway-funky-dancing trees. This time they were to keep their blindfolds off so that they could see clearly.

Minty the Crocodile felt snappy after taking the wrong turn before. He was determined to win this time as he sized up the competition. Among the newcomers were an ostrich, a chipmunk with big bushy eyebrows, a walrus, a pelican, a skunk, a few grasshoppers, and of course the wolf cubs.

Watch Out!

The starter whistle was blown and they were off! First they had to run through an orchard and along a grass track with curvy bends. Then they had to climb up a steep hill and down the other side. Next came Prickle Lane; a mass of sleeping hedgehogs lying on a sandy path. When the ostrich saw the hedgehogs he stopped, gasped with horror and dunked his head in the sand, sending his chipmunk passenger flying, backside first, onto the hedgehogs' spikes.

"Ha!" squawked Pearl the Hawk chuckling. "I must remember to tell the others not to bury their heads in the sand like the Ostrich. We're not supposed to hide our feelings when we come across something that upsets us."

Pearl jumped up and down with pure pleasure when she saw that most of her friends were instinctively finding different ways to go round the Hedgehogs.

"Yes! Yes!" thought Pearl to herself, "It instinctively feels good to Clay to dig under the Hedgehogs but it feels much better to Sunny to step over them! When you do what feels best to you, you're following the Navigator's guidance! Only *you* can instinctively feel what's best for *you* to do! *No one else* can check your feelings for you!" She watched the Grasshoppers looking ahead and then springing back a few paces, then they turned around to take massive steps towards the Hedgehogs, and one huge bounce to clear them.

The Skunk, who was bringing up the rear, sprayed her scent as soon as she set eyes on Prickle Lane. The unbelievable stench rapidly cleared the spectators and also sent the Hedgehogs running, giving the stinky Skunk a clear passage to skip on through.

Although Minty was in the lead, and he was determined to win, his oomph was beginning to fade. The race was good fun but he felt that he needed to pace himself, so he stopped to rest his weary paws before steaming ahead again.

He did well to pay attention to his feelings by taking a rest, because from where he was sitting he could watch his friends pass through Pearl's next hazardous surprise, which was the Coconut Trail.

The racers had to duck and dive to avoid the coconut cannon balls that were being fired at them. Minty was cunning enough to work out the order in which the coconuts were being fired. He stood up, took a few deep breaths and proudly scampered through completely unharmed.

As they neared the finish line, the contestants were surprised by a different type of obstacle. As each runner passed a big group of trees with overhanging branches, the trees barked, "Watch Out!"

Some of the animals, including a few of the Rainbow Surfers, looked terrified and froze on the spot, cowering uneasily as they looked around. At that point the trees were instructed to splash the participants with the buckets of water they were holding in their swaying branches. Any soaked contestant was automatically disqualified from the race.

Several Rainbow Surfers, including Minty, who had been following behind the rest, were now turning the corner on the race track, about to pass the same group of trees. Again, they were unsuspecting when they heard the trees yell "Watch Out!" But rather than being worried, these Rainbow Surfers looked around eagerly, full of excitement at discovering something wonderful.

Minty peered between the trees and saw Sarah, a beautiful Lady Crocodile sunbathing on the riverbank some way past the finish line. He sometimes wished that he had a crocodile friend to do things with. His Rainbow Surfer friends were fantastic, but it wasn't always enough, and they didn't understand about being a crocodile. Spurred on, he never took his eyes off the lovely crocodile. She looks friendly too, he thought. With an added spring in his step, he rushed forward to meet her. He whistled as he passed the finish post first, wiggling and waggling his tail, and punching the air with pride.

Minty opened his mouth to say hello to Sarah, but no sound came out. He moved closer, fumbling in his pocket and pulled out a tasty fish that he had been keeping in reserve. He drop kicked it on his back foot, which sent it flying high in the air. With one snap Sarah, the Lady Crocodile, caught and swallowed it. Impressive, he thought. He nodded at her as he stumbled slightly and went on his way, suddenly feeling shy and not knowing what to do or say. So he said and did nothing.

The Movie Screen in Minty's Mind

Minty felt annoyed at himself for not saying anything to the Lady Crocodile. Slowly he sauntered over to meet up with the other Rainbow Surfers, who had started dancing to the latest cool tunes at The Boogie Garden again. He decided to keep quiet about hoping to be friends with the Lady Crocodile as he thought that his Rainbow Surfer friends might not understand that sometimes he felt lonely.

A few hours later they decided to set off again in their LightShips.

With nightfall approaching, Clay the Badger spotted a sign for Diva's Jungle. The air was still warm as the sun set but it was time to rest and they decided to moor up. They soon found an inviting cave beautifully lit by glow-worms where they could settle down to close their eyes. Snuggled together, they drifted off to sleep. That is, all except Minty the Crocodile.

He tossed and turned, still annoyed with himself. "Why didn't I stop and talk to that Lady Crocodile? How impressively she caught the fish. I bet we'd have so much fun together and oh how I wanted a crocodile friend! Now I never will! Oh I'm such an idiot!" he thought angrily.

Minty the Crocodile didn't usually say very much, so he sometimes gave the impression that he was not very loving. Yet he had a huge heart, even if he was a little snappy at times.

Booster the Lion had been woken up by a kicking foot, and as he lay there in the dark, he sensed Minty's anguish.

"Oh what a mess!" grumbled Minty. Then he turned to Booster to ask, "If I had asked a new friend to come with us, do you think she would have shared my LightShip?"

"If she came with you, she'd have her own LightShip. You'd sail together; on different ships, but together, just like the rest of us," offered a voice in the darkness.

"Oh," sighed Minty sadly, "My Navigator has really let me down!"

"What?" asked Booster.

"I'm so fed up! Well, I asked it to help me find a crocodile friend. I can't see myself ever finding one now!" He spluttered furiously through gritted teeth, turning his face to hide his moist eyes.

"The Navigator didn't let you down; you let yourself down." remarked Booster the Lion. "If you can't *see* yourself sailing along with a crocodile friend, it's not going to happen. So how did you dream about it happening?"

"Oh! I just dreamt of meeting her…Er yes, and I guess that's all that happened!" muttered Minty quietly, somewhat stunned as he realized that he had needed to do more than that.

Pearl the Hawk suggested, "Try dreaming about meeting AND chatting AND sailing off with your crocodile friend to make sure that everything works out the way you want it to.

But remember, the crocodile friend of your dreams may not be the one you think it is. So be open to meeting up with someone new."

Minty the Crocodile asked, "Well then how am I supposed to know if I've chosen the right friend for me?"

Booster the Lion reckoned the treasured golden coin was bound to have the answer so he propped himself up and took it out of his pocket, "Take a look!" he said as he threw it over to Minty. Again the words had slightly changed but the meaning was, as always, still the same.

Upside of FEELING GOOD about those around you:

When you want new friends, smile at others, as your smile will be returned to you!

When you look at what you like, it always feels better than when you look at something you don't like. So when you look at others, always look for what you like in them, because that will pull you into a genuinely better mood.

If it feels better to look at something or someone different, then keep following this guidance, as it will lead you to the good experiences you want and the desires you dream about!

Downside of FEELING BAD about those around you:

When you look at things you don't like, it never feels good. So when you're full of anger, hatred or revenge, when you criticize, judge, or when you're nasty to yourself or to others, deep inside it doesn't feel good.

When you don't feel good and you are moving away from your dreams and desires, aim to find ways of feeling better. The better you feel, the faster you go towards what you want and the quicker you arrive!

Minty placed the coin on the ground and laid his head next to it as he repeated to himself… **When you feel bad you are moving away from what you want, so keep focusing on what feels good as that will lead you to the desires you dream about!** He closed his eyes and started dreaming about what he really wanted to happen. He did feel better. Soon afterwards he fell into a deep sleep.

The next morning, the group of friends explored their new surroundings. They had a wonderful day and by the time nightfall came, they had discovered a new cave to snooze in. Amid tired yawns, most of the Rainbow Surfers settled down to rest, whilst Chatty the Frog tiptoed outside the cave to find a quiet spot on her own. She crouched down and hid under a big leaf in the moonlight. She glanced up at the star-filled sky and then over towards some long shadows by the river.

In the half-light she felt cold. She sat there worrying about having to let her friends down as she prepared to tell them her secret in the morning.

CHAPTER

Views at Diva's Jungle

After a seemingly endless night, the dawn chorus started to welcome the new day. Chatty was still crouched under the big leaf, listening to the snoring coming from the cave that almost drowned out the beautiful bird song. The songbirds turned up the volume of their wake-up call but the snoring continued until one of the more brightly-coloured birds flew into the cave and landed heavily on Clay the Badger, who was using Sunny the Giraffe's chubby tummy as her warm pillow.

The songbird poked Clay's back sharply with her beak a few times and twanged her eyebrows before screeching in a huff "C'mon you lot! Wake up! Wake up!" Clay was too comfy to open her eyes or to move from her cozy spot. Then, the songbird hopped onto the ground next to Booster the Lion's nose. She tugged on his ear with all her might, chirping persistently, until she got his attention. Booster growled as he stretched over and bashed the singing alarm clock. Horrified, Clay sprung open her eyes to see the bird looking somewhat crumpled.

Clay the Badger gasped and sat up in stunned silence. She was about to bend over to pick up the dazed songbird when she saw that he was pushing himself up. The songbird then stumbled, staggered, and stormed out of the cave while grumbling under his breath. He shook his head as he stomped past a cockerel, who had also overslept but who was now beginning to stir.

The cockerel quickly made up for lost time by also starting up his morning call. This startled Minty the Crocodile who dug his claws in to what he thought was a soft cushion next to him. Clay gulped; her eyes bulged out as Minty's claws sunk deep into her fur. She tapped him with some force! He opened his eyes in bleary surprise and then he quickly removed his clasp from her knee.

Roused from their slumber, the friends came out of the cave stretching and yawning, squinting in the daylight. Chatty the Frog peeped out from under the big leaf and slowly hopped forward. One by one her friends greeted her with their usual light pat on her head, which meant that her head seemed to recoil down to her toes and bounce back up again. This was the morning that Chatty had dreaded and her eyes welled up with tears. She felt cold and sweaty, her heart was pounding and her webbed hands were clammy.

She could feel a lump in her throat as she asked her friends to sit down and listen. She felt scared as she croaked and sniffed. She was absentmindedly fiddling with the head of a wildflower. Time was dragging until finally she plucked up the courage to tell the group that she thought she had a disease in one of her eyes and it was making it hard for her to see clearly.

Sunny the Giraffe was feeling very sure of himself, having taken the time to really understand how their feelings give them the Navigator's guidance. He stepped in front of Chatty the Frog and swung his long neck down to her legs, then he stretched it around to her back and then back to her front again, so that his big brown eyes with their long, slow-blinking eyelashes appeared directly in front of her face.

"What? What? What are you looking for?" whined Chatty, sniffling.

"I know you're upset, but I'm looking for your sense of humor," replied Sunny.

"Are you out of your mind?" Chatty the Frog replied.

"Yes I am. I'm out of my mind, and into my feelings," said Sunny with a soft tone in his voice. He paused for what seemed like ages and then he said calmly, "You can be healthy again if you want to be! **Never fix your sights on what you don't want but on what you DO want so that your LightShip automatically has to take you there.**"

"Haven't you heard a word I've said?" exploded Chatty the Frog, fighting back her fury.

"Oh! You sound hopping mad!" provoked Sunny.

"Yup, and that's not funny either!" cried out Chatty, pounding a clump of moss next to her with her clenched webbed fist.

"Come on, lighten up!" replied Sunny.

"Huh? How can you be so mean to me? " By now Chatty was outraged.

She rose to her full height, put her webbed hands on her hips and leaned towards Sunny. But Sunny spoke first, "No, not mean! A few moments ago you were stuck in self-pity. Now you've got some fire back in your belly!"

Chatty grimaced. Suddenly she yelled up at Sunny, "Why can't you accept the facts? Face reality! My eye hurts. You'll have to go on without me!"

"How does that thought make you feel?" he asked.

Chatty frowned.

Pearl added, **"Yes, try to think thoughts that make you feel good so that you'll be following your Navigator's guidance to wherever you want to go!** You want to get back to full health and it can take you there."

Without a second thought, Chatty the Frog punched Pearl the Hawk on the beak.

Shocked, the group stared in stunned silence, first at Chatty and then at their wounded friend. Chatty winced when she realized what she had done, and apologized awkwardly with tears running down her face. She added quickly, "It's easy for you to say do this and do that. I'm the one who's hurting! Ouch! Now my hand aches as well! Ooh, I'm sorry I hit you." She flicked her wrist in an effort to shake off the pain.

Pearl the Hawk rubbed her beak with both wings. "That's okay," she murmured out of the side of her squished beak.

Clay the Badger looked towards Sunny the Giraffe and asked, "Can we do anything to help?"

He replied, "All we can do is help her think about things that makes her feel better." He paused and then said, "But how she feels is up to her."

Chatty overheard them talking, wiped a tear with one webbed hand and her runny nose with the other, "I hope you're not saying I'm to blame for this! This is not my fault!"

Pearl was still rubbing her beak as she replied, "It's not about being anyone's fault. **Blame makes you feel awful and takes you totally off course again. However terrible things may seem, they're only temporary. That's all. Whatever your situation, it can be improved! It really can be!"**

Sunny the Giraffe suddenly had the urge to stretch his legs. He stood up to his full height and in the distance he saw a shrub with its powerfully nutritious fruit. He remembered that it could be made into a medicinal tonic that could soothe and heal many ailments. "Now there's a good thought!" he said to himself.

The mist was rising and beginning to roll along the valley. Chatty wanted to be by herself, so the others decided to go in search of the healing fruit.

Left alone, Chatty the Frog wept as she stomped her webbed feet in fury and kicked a pile of loose stones, sending them flying. As soon as she had kicked them, she regretted it; when the little stones had scattered they left a large sharply-edged rock underneath and she hurt her webbed foot on its side.

"Can it get any worse?" she shouted out, clutching her aching wrist and lifting her foot off the ground to ease the pain.

Why me?

Shoulders drooping, Chatty the Frog sobbed as she limped over to huddle under a canopy of old leaves by a gushing waterfall. The morning dew had gone and dark clouds were forming overhead.

When the tears that had been streaming down her cheeks ran dry, she cried out "Why? Why did this have to happen to me?"

That reminded her of a few things she had been told a while back: **"If you have angry thoughts then you'll become angrier, and if you have sad thoughts then you'll become sadder. By finding ways of feeling better about everything that happens today, you improve what you attract into your life tomorrow.**

When something makes you feel bad, it isn't the situation itself but rather how you are thinking about the situation that makes you feel like that.

So, if you change how you look at what has happened, you change how it feels to you. That's because if you have happy thoughts you'll be happier, and if you have healthy thoughts you'll be healthier.

We all see a different world, and our world is a reflection of who we are. When we change our thoughts, we change our feelings and we change our world…we change *THE* World!"

Chatty the Frog reflected on all this for a while. If she continued to think about all her worries, then she would certainly end up becoming even more worried. She suddenly understood that at every single moment she had the choice of what she thought about.

Chatty stood up and looked left, looked right and then looked down. She scratched her head and sat down again. Then she turned around and looked behind her. She was in exactly the same spot, but she had a new and different point of view, in more ways than one!

"It's NEVER too late to change my mind. Yes! Yes! Yes! And as soon as I do, I change my direction and my destination! Ha!" She shouted impulsively, banging her webbed hand on her head, "Of course! How obvious!" she yelled out.

She did want to be well again. She knew that it would be unrealistic to expect herself to jump from despair to total happiness but even if the change in her mood was very gradual, it had to be better than the terrified feelings she had been having. It made sense that being frozen with fear was going to keep her stuck in her problems and being scared to death was not going to help her get better!

Chatty was deep in thought when she heard her friends return. Her lips curved into a huge smile and her face brightened as she saw them arrive.

The Return

Their paws were overloaded. Not only had they brought back the shrub's fruit to make into a medicinal juice for her, but they had also collected lots of other gifts. Each of the Rainbow Surfers took a turn in placing their presents in front of Chatty and giving her a softer version of their usual friendly greeting by fondly patting her lightly on her head. They wanted her to know how much they cared and how much they wanted her to be well again.

Pearl the Hawk unfolded her vast wingspan and pulled Chatty into a feathery hug. It felt safe and comforting to Chatty who closed her eyes as she soaked up the affection. When she opened them she saw Minty the Crocodile smiling and winking at her, which made her chuckle.

Clay the Badger stepped closer and placed her soft paws on Chatty's shoulders to squeeze them gently before giving her a gentle kiss on the forehead. Booster the Lion bounded forward playfully and mopped up her happy tears with a big sloppy lick. Chatty was so surprised that she began to laugh with her friends, shrugging off her worries and forgetting her problems.

Clay the Badger started tickling Chatty the Frog from behind while singing light-heartedly,

"We squeeze and tease you. We huddle to cuddle you." The overjoyed Chatty croaked with delight. Giggling turned into fits of laughter as they rolled around playfully tickling and tackling each other. Soon everyone started laughing, their happy noises echoing throughout the jungle.

Iris the Butterfly, who had been resting on a nearby nettle with her wings spread towards the sun, was enjoying the warm glow of loving feelings amongst her friends. She flew down to join in the fun. Clay the Badger started tickling her as well and soon afterwards Iris' antennae were shaking with laughter as she tumbled backwards on the ground, legs in the air, clutching her tummy while belly laughing.

Soon afterwards the friends happily united in a loving circle to show that they were on their journey together as one.

Recovery

In her own time, Chatty the Frog began to feel a lot happier and even more determined to be well again. She grasped just how powerful her thoughts and feelings were, so she took the time to appreciate everything around her much more. That way she was thinking good thoughts, which made her feel wonderful, and the result was that she began enjoying herself a lot more too. It felt so much better, and so much more fun, than always complaining about everything (including the weather) as she used to do.

If it were raining, she felt good that the plants were having a drink so that the land would stay green and colourful. If it were stormy, she enjoyed the smell of freshness in the air and the fast moving display of clouds in the sky. If it were windy, she flew a kite and if it were sunny she would enjoy the warmth on her eyelids as she sunbathed.

She thought about as many different reasons to feel happy as she could and decided to be grateful that she was able to see out of her eyes at all, even if it was a little blurry on one side. She began to appreciate every moment when she had no pain, which was usually when she was thinking about other things.

When she felt sad or afraid, she asked her Navigator what she should do. She would ask by thinking about various options and then, by deciding which option felt the best, she would know the Navigator's guidance. Sometimes it felt best to her to go and have a little snooze on her own, or to drink more of the medicinal juice, and at other times it just felt good to have fun with her friends.

She relied more and more on her Navigator's advice in this way. She understood that anything that felt right to her, whether it was taking extra rest or visiting the local medicine expert or drinking the juice, meant that she was on her way back towards full health again.

She gratefully noticed that her eye was beginning to feel more comfortable every day. **The more grateful she was, the better she felt. She was heading right for her desire and she knew it!** She hopped over to her friends and said, "I bet I know what's going to be on our golden coin if I take a look at it now. Let me see it! Who has it?" Chatty reached out her webbed hand towards her pals and Minty the Crocodile delved into his pocket and then gave it to her.

Upside of FEELING GOOD about what you communicate:

Just as you choose to listen to the music you like because it makes you feel good, choose to think thoughts that you like, as they will make you feel good too. The better you feel, the faster you go towards what you want and the quicker you arrive!

Downside of FEELING BAD about what you communicate:

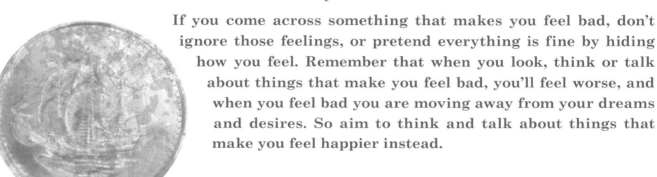

If you come across something that makes you feel bad, don't ignore those feelings, or pretend everything is fine by hiding how you feel. Remember that when you look, think or talk about things that make you feel bad, you'll feel worse, and when you feel bad you are moving away from your dreams and desires. So aim to think and talk about things that make you feel happier instead.

"Ha! I thought so! Yes! I've got it! Rather than worrying about the problem with my eye, I was right in thinking about anything else that makes me feel a little better! Soon I'll be totally healthy again, you'll see!" exclaimed Chatty the Frog gleefully.

It took a little time, but Chatty's eye healed well. In fact it became healthier than her other one! While the locals said it was a miracle, the Rainbow Surfers knew that it was simply the natural outcome of Chatty's new choice of direction.

Chatty the Frog was ready to leave with her friends and continue on their journey.

CHAPTER

The Cocoon

The Rainbow Surfers climbed back into their LightShips and were eager to keep sailing on to find The Krystal Kavern. As they sailed past some hippos, Chatty the Frog found the going so easy now that she wondered why she had had such a hard time moving her ship in the past.

After a while, they arrived at an interesting-looking jetty and decided to stop and take a look around. As Booster the Lion approached, he bumped his LightShip into a snoozing hippo. Rubbing his head, the hippo slowly raised himself out of the sparkling water. Liquid silver mud was dripping down his sleepy face. Grumpily he snorted, "I say, watch what you're doing, chum!" after which he sank back into his comfy waterbed.

Some colourful Dragonflies whizzed close to snoop inside Iris the Butterfly's LightShip, their gemstone-covered wings flickering in the sunlight. Once their curiosity was satisfied, the Dragonflies flew back to the riverside and beckoned the Rainbow Surfers to join them.

"Where are we please?" Booster the Lion inquired.

The youngest Dragonfly buzzed back that the name of their hometown was "The Silver Grotto."

Booster shot an excited look towards Minty the Crocodile. Minty remembered Booster saying that he had wanted to be wealthy, so he commented, "Nice name! Sound's like somewhere worth investigating!"

"Yes The Silver Grotto!" replied Booster the Lion, his ears pricking up with interest. He soon became just as curious about the Dragonflies' Silver Grotto as the Dragonflies had been about their LightShips. After all, The Silver Grotto had gemstone-covered silver fruit and the crops were ripe and ready for picking!

As they came ashore, the friends' paws and tails swished and sloshed around in the warm sloppy silver mud as they squelched their way to the firmer diamond-coated rocks. Off to the left was a silver geyser. The steaming, silver liquid spurted high into the air, making a wide arc before falling sharply, causing rippling waves that glittered in the sun. Shimmering bubbles in the gleaming mud were continuously brewing, bursting and popping.

The Dragonflies were admiring Iris the Butterfly's stunning wings when Grandma Dragonfly commented, "Your wings are really beautiful. We often forget what you butterflies have to go through. When the caterpillar thinks her world is coming to an end, she becomes a butterfly. It's quite inspiring!"

As the sun began to set, Iris remembered her caterpillar days. In her heart she always knew that she was meant to do more than just crawl along the ground or make her way slowly up a stem to take a bite out of a leaf. She knew she could fly. She would lie for hours in the cool grass, looking up at the sky, picturing herself drifting gracefully from flower to flower. However, if she mentioned her dream to any of the other worms and bugs down on her level they would shake their heads and say, "Tsk, tsk. Who do you think you are? Don't dream too big!"

Still, Iris knew deep down what she wanted to become. One day a handsome butterfly settled on a blade of grass near where she was crawling. Iris found the nerve to speak to the gorgeous creature. She looked up at him keenly before asking, "Were you always able to fly like that?"

The butterfly, whose name was Stripey, replied, "Ah, no. I used to be a caterpillar like you."

Iris was so excited that she trembled as she asked, "But how did you do it? How did you go from being a caterpillar to becoming a butterfly?"

Stripey flapped his wings a few times and said, "Do you know much about cocoons?"

Iris nodded slowly, "A little. Why do you ask?"

"That's your answer," said Stripey with a wink and a warm smile. "In your cocoon you relax for a while, and you always feel better when you relax. The better you feel the more inspired you'll become and the quicker you'll achieve all that you want!"

Rather than being confused about why she had to go into a cocoon, Iris started looking forward to it. When it was time, she remembered his words. She also remembered to keep loving herself as a caterpillar, whilst keeping her mind fixed on what she wanted to become...a beautiful butterfly. Wonderful ideas came to her when she relaxed in her cocoon, and when she finally felt her wings lift her off the ground, it was the best feeling ever – even better than she had imagined it would be!

Since then, Iris the Butterfly always took some time every day to relax on her own. It always made her feel better and she knew it would help allow great ideas to flow to her either then or later. She smiled with happiness as she tapped the upside of the treasured golden coin with the tip of her wing as she read the words on it.

Upside of resting is FEELING GOOD and allowing wonderful ideas to come to mind:

Take time to relax everyday because when you relax, you always feel better and that's when wonderful ideas flow to you. As you think about things that pull you into a genuinely better mood, you are being drawn to the good things you want and to the desires you dream about!

Downside of not resting is FEELING BAD and having less ideas come to mind:

When you rush around all the time without taking time to rest and relax you become tired and then great ideas don't flow so well and you don't feel so good. When you feel bad and you are moving away from your dreams and desires, aim to find ways of feeling better. The better you feel, the faster you go towards what you want and the quicker you arrive!

The Dragonflies were intrigued by Iris's story and by the golden coin she was holding. As a thank you in return for the story, a Dragonfly named John offered to take everyone to his secret hideout. He jumped up and shook a light layering of silver dust off his wings, which sparkled as it sprinkled to the ground. Then he spun up into the air. The other Dragonflies copied his ritual and were soon flying off as well. John the Dragonfly turned back to the Rainbow Surfers and shouted out, "Follow me!"

The Hideout

John the Dragonfly led the group past canyons with stunning views from the cliffs down into lush valleys with vibrant, tropical jungles.

The ground beneath them was covered with colourful wildflowers, and sunlight glinted off the Dragonflies' wings.

Every now and again, Grandma Dragonfly flew slower and lower than the rest. Whenever John the Dragonfly noticed, he gave a signal to one of the others to give her a lift for a while. This plan worked until a couple of the more playful dragonflies, Matthew and Harry, started their dive-bombing game.

For a moment Grandma Dragonfly seemed suspended in mid-air as she considered her options. Then she decided to hitch a lift with her new friend, Chatty the Frog. Chatty was completely amazed that any Dragonfly would choose her as a companion. She wanted to repay the honour by providing a smooth ride. Every time Chatty took a hop forward, Grandma Dragonfly bounced even higher. Chatty peered over her shoulder to make sure Grandma Dragonfly landed back on her shoulder safely before taking her next hop. She resisted the temptation to make huge splashes in the puddles that she passed on the way.

John the Dragonfly led them to an incredible place. They were high above a valley and as the collection of animals and insects lined up to look at the view, there was no space left for Chatty and Grandma Dragonfly. They tried to look over the others' shoulders but they could not see a thing. Feeling left out, Grandma Dragonfly's antennae drooped sadly. But as they began feeling upset, Chatty the Frog remembered her experience with her eye.

She remembered to let her feelings guide her thoughts. So rather than staying put and feeling sad, she looked around to find something that would make her feel better. Suddenly she felt inspired. She told Grandma Dragonfly to hold on tightly as she took one leap on the ground, the second on Minty's back and a third leap that took them up to a rock positioned high above the others' heads. Feeling rather pleased with themselves, they ended up with the best view of all!

Before them lay vast rolling fields of buttercups. Cutting through the middle was a long dark grey pathway. The Rainbow Surfers glanced at each other, baffled by what they saw. Floating above the path were thousands of stunning bubbles, all the colours of the rainbow. Some drifted aimlessly while others darted forward at great speed. Some were bumping into each other or stuck by the side of the road.

Every time John the Dragonfly had come to this secret hideaway he had been fascinated, but not sure what to make of it all. He whispered, "What's going on down there? Do you have any ideas?"

"Ah yes!" said Pearl the Hawk, impressed by what she saw. "Those are Thought Bubbles," she replied.

Everyone looked puzzled. Pearl went on, "Those bubbles are full of the thoughts of everyone around here.

See how some of the bubbles are going in a straight line, moving powerfully ahead? Well, they are the thoughts of those who are focused on their desires and who are being guided by the Navigator to stay on track. At night **when you're 'in the dark' the Thought Bubbles shine their light wherever you place your attention, so it's quite clear where you're heading!**

See the bubbles that have tumbled off the path? Those are thoughts that come from fear." Clay the Badger swallowed hard and nodded when she heard this, remembering her own mishap with her LightShip at the beginning of their adventure.

"And the bubbles that are sort of bobbing along aimlessly," Pearl continued, "they are the vacant thoughts that have no direction." Sunny the Giraffe gulped in amazement as he saw that those drifting bubbles were mostly the same yellow as his section of the rainbow. By now, all of the Rainbow Surfers were staring hard at the bubbles.

Pearl then added, **"You see the long windy road ahead? It represents your journey and that it unfolds as you go along, so there's no need to worry that you don't know what's around the next corner because that's what makes the journey so exciting!"**

They watched in awe for a while and then chatted excitedly as they left the hideout. They made their way back to the jetty at the The Silver Grotto where their LightShips were moored. As they sauntered along, Sunny the Giraffe had a good munch on some of their scrumptious silver coated leaves.

Before departing, Booster the Lion filled his LightShip with bags bulging with gifts of the gemstone-silver fruit that the generous Dragonflies had invited him to pick.

As they took off down the River of Life, Pearl the Hawk took her time surveying the scenery around her. The friends were laughing and calling out to each other as they easily sailed forward. It wasn't long before Pearl yelled out to the others to moor their ships because she had spotted something intriguing between the trees.

CHAPTER

The Krystal Kavern!

As the Rainbow Surfers moored, they caught the smell of spices wafting towards them from the Toy Palace on Spice Island. All the friends except Clay the Badger and Sunny the Giraffe ventured inland towards a magnificent building with great marble towers that shone in the morning sun. They made their way in and found soft cushions to sit on amongst the life-size toys.

Clay was worried. She was afraid that Sunny the Giraffe had been left behind. How would he find them? Maybe he'd fallen in the river? Rather than joining her friends for some fun with the life-size toys, she was sitting on the bank of the river staring anxiously upstream, waiting to catch sight of him. She tapped her claws against the jetty, but fretting would not make him arrive any sooner. **She had a choice, she could worry that the worst might have happened or she could be hopeful that something good might have happened to him instead.**

She remembered that Pearl the Hawk had said, "If you worry about the past or the future, it means you'll be missing out on the fun you could be having now. And since life is made up of a whole load of 'NOWs,' it seems a shame to miss them! **When you're having fun, you automatically stop worrying.** It's the perfect answer!"

She stood up, scratched her head and then brushed down her fur. Clay the Badger smiled proudly to herself for changing her thoughts so that she felt better. Then she turned around and made her way over to the soft cushions where the others were playing. Some birds windsurfed overhead and Clay looked up. As she looked back down she saw Sunny the Giraffe coming around the last bend in the river, his LightShip filled to the brim with a plentiful supply of a new variety of leaves.

He had been delayed because he had felt like stretching his legs a bit earlier than the others and so had moored up and gone for a wander. Whilst enjoying his new surroundings, he had noticed some interesting looking trees that he had never seen before and to his great delight he found that they had the most heavenly tasting leaves. He filled his LightShip with plenty of them and then continued on his way to meet up with his friends. He waved at Clay the Badger as he chomped on some of the brightest green ones from his collection.

Sunny disembarked in time to meet Sam the Penguin, the waiter who had come to give the Rainbow Surfers an extraordinary invitation.

Celebrating Today

The friends were being invited to a grand banquet. They followed Sam the Penguin to a large hall to join a party sitting at a long wooden table. The flickering log fire glowing behind them cast moving shadows and oak-scented puffs of smoke floated gently towards them.

It was "TODAY" on Spice Island and everyone was celebrating. The Rainbow Surfers looked around excitedly. Minty the Crocodile was not sure what to make of the Iguana whom he saw out of the corner of his eye. She was checking her outfit in a long mirror, and then, seeing the group, came and sat down next to him.

Moments later Minty was being pushed from behind, as Nick the Hippo came around clumsily to top up their glasses. He seemed distracted and refilled the glasses with a different drink. Minty looked down into his glass and scrunched up his nose at the weird-looking concoction that was fizzing wildly inside it. He glanced up to see Booster the Lion smirking back at him and they burst out laughing.

Booster spotted Sam the Penguin close by and asked, "What's so special about TODAY?"

"Oh, Today is very special. We intend to enjoy every single moment of it. It only comes once in a lifetime!" came back the reply.

"So what is today?"

"Well, Today *is* Today! It's the present moment, never to be seen again. The most amazing times happen in the present moment and it's so easy to let'em pass you by unnoticed, you know!"

"Great reason for a party!" said Booster, raising his glass and extending it towards Minty's until both glasses met with a cheery clinking noise.

After the banquet, Sam the Penguin invited the Rainbow Surfers to hear a band called Slurp downstairs at The Krystal Kavern.

"Nah, we don't want to go there," said Booster the Lion cockily, thinking that Sam the Penguin was joking.

The others gasped and stared open-mouthed in disbelief.

Chatty the Frog was speechless. Alarmed, she looked sideways at Booster the Lion and then back at the waiter as she stuttered and croaked, "What? It's here? The Krystal Kavern is here?"

Everyone turned around and stared at the waiter with excited anticipation.

When Booster the Lion realized that the waiter had not been joking after all, he quickly retracted his words. "Well, actually... er...yes...we would like to go in, please."

Sam the Penguin nodded and smiled as he began to usher the group of friends towards the stairs leading down to the entrance of The Krystal Kavern. The Rainbow Surfers could hardly contain their excitement. This was it!

"Oh my goodness! Oh my goodness!" Clay the Badger shouted.

"Wow, we've made it! We've arrived!" exclaimed Chatty the Frog, hopping up and down. "We're here! We're really here!"

Sam the Penguin waited patiently as the friends celebrated together. He was used to visitors being so excited that they had found The Krystal Kavern. Finally, he led the group to the entrance. When they reached it, Booster the Lion leapt down the marble staircase first, calling out, "C'mon! Let's find out what's so special about this place!" The others followed on behind.

Minty the Crocodile savored every moment as he stepped down the broad staircase alongside Clay the Badger, following their noses towards the intriguing scent coming from the elegant candle-lit seating area below.

The walls of The Krystal Kavern rose high over their heads. They glittered and sparkled in the flickering candlelight. A thousand arches formed by stalactites and stalagmites divided the sides of the cave into mysterious areas, all lit by candles. Everywhere the walls sparkled with crystals catching the light, like the sun twinkling on clear water. It was breathtaking.

The Rainbow Surfers were offered cups filled with smooth hot nectar and they carefully took sips as they walked towards the middle of the cave, where a chocolate fountain overflowed, forming little warm chocolate pools on the floor.

The Surfing Rainbows Golden Intention Code

Clay the Badger scooped up a few delicious drops of chocolate and playfully plopped them on Booster the Lion's nose. Smiling, he wiped them off as they continued to look around the cave.

Minty the Crocodile admired the polished tables that were carved out of beautiful wood and were surrounded by chairs covered in deep red velvet. Each table had a mound of chocolates piled into a crystal bowl. There was golden caramel in creamy milk chocolate; nuts and raisins hidden in truffles; vanilla fudge topped with nougat; fresh strawberries coated in a rich dark chocolate; butter toffee and honey in a crunchy chocolate honeycomb.

The group of friends looked around for a while, soaking up the atmosphere. Clay the Badger entered a side cave filled with crystals that seemed to have a special light inside them. She felt moved to touch one of these crystals and watched as it grew until it was as tall as she was. As the crystal became clearer, she jumped back in surprise.

Reflected in the crystal was Clay the Badger as she truly was, beautiful, peaceful and full of trust. Clay blinked hard and smiled at the image, which smiled back at her. With a slight movement of her head, the image indicated to Clay that she should touch the next crystal. An image appeared in that one as well. This time, Clay saw herself as she once was, having just climbed up the riverbank after falling in the water. Clay smiled at herself, with her wet fur and sorry face. Immediately that image faded and she was left with her real, radiant self again.

One by one the other Rainbow Surfers entered the Crystal Room. They all had the same experience. Sunny the Giraffe laughed happily at his image. He saw himself with a smart captain's hat positioned proudly on his head, happily knowing how to flip his feelings from disappointment to cheerful anticipation whenever aiming for new treasures, such as finding his collection of tasty leaves.

Booster the Lion saw a self-confident lion with a magnificent mane surrounded by great wealth, and Minty the Crocodile saw himself with many crocodile friends and he felt his own heart overflow. Chatty the Frog was chitchatting joyfully about her fully healed eyes and Iris the Butterfly was elated by the inspiring thoughts that filled her mind after her daily relaxing time.

The group of friends looked around when Pearl the Hawk entered the room and they gasped at the heavenly light coming from her crystal and the beautiful image of her sailing easily in her LightShip.

Enchanted by what they had just seen in the crystals, they set off to explore the other parts of The Krystal Kavern.

The ever-hungry Minty the Crocodile was curious to try the treats, so he looked around for a large table with plenty of room for the others to join him later. By the time the others arrived, he was finishing a cup of hot nectar and was listening to the saxophone being played by the band on stage. Looking over the rim of his cup, Minty smiled and waved to greet his friends. He had a nectar smile from ear to ear!

As his friends sat down at the table, they also tucked into the various treats. Soon afterwards Chatty the Frog, who had still been exploring The Krystal Kavern on her own, rushed over to the table, balancing a big book in her arms.

"What have you got there? Let's see," said Pearl the Hawk, reaching out her wings to help with the book. Rays of bright white light came streaming out as Pearl began to open it. They were so bright that she almost dropped it as she quickly shut it again. Slowly Pearl the Hawk opened up the book once again. She seemed to be able to see deep into her own soul within the light that shone back at her.

A few scrolls fell from the book and Booster the Lion picked them up and gasped as he saw the words "The Promise of Surfing Rainbows" written in fancy bold ink. Clasping the sheets between his big trembling paws he carefully passed them back to Pearl, but she made a gesture that he should keep hold of them.

Booster the Lion felt very important. The others watched in silence as he cleared his throat and started to read the text of the glowing words.

The Promise of Surfing Rainbows

When you are Surfing Rainbows, you are harnessing the powerful ancient wisdom that helps you attract your desires to you.

They sat back in stunned silence.

"What's Surfing Rainbows?" asked Minty the Crocodile curiously.

Pearl the Hawk decided that now was the time to explain what she had known all along. "Take another look at the golden coin that we found amongst the treasure at the end of our rainbow," she said as she passed it to him, and he then began to study the words carefully.

Upside of FEELING GOOD:

You really can be awake when you experience your dreams!

When you think about things that pull you into a genuinely better mood, you are being drawn to the good things that you want to happen and to whatever you dream about!

Downside of FEELING BAD:

Feeling bad about anything sends you off course.

So when you feel bad and you are moving away from your dreams and desires, aim to find ways of feeling better. The better you feel, the faster you go towards what you want and the quicker you arrive!

Minty the Crocodile gave the coin back to Pearl the Hawk while giving her an inquiring look. She smiled and said, **"The LightShips are an illusion; they are an extension of us. You are your own LightShip and the Navigator is always with you, wherever you are.**

You see, the direction of your thoughts, indicated to you by your feelings, has always controlled the direction in which you travel in life and so whether or not you are heading towards a life you'll love living. Most don't realize it and neither did we until we started out on this trip.

The LightShip was just a vehicle to make it clear how important and how powerful our thoughts and feelings really are, because when on board that's the only thing that made them move."

"Hmm," nodded Minty pensively. "But if I don't have a LightShip then how can the Navigator help me?"

"The Navigator always talks to you through your feelings. But, rather than you being taken somewhere in your LightShip, what actually happens when you follow your Navigator's guidance is that you are attracting everything you need to make things work out well for you. It may seem as though you have more 'lucky' breaks, or feel inspired to act on some good ideas. All sorts of things will happen like that to help you fulfill your goals."

Pearl the Hawk continued, **"However bad your current situation and whatever the problem you may find yourself in, always look for anything that you can be grateful for. Even if you are grateful for something small like the shelter where you sleep, stop, take a moment and feel good about it. Then look for something else to feel good about, and then something else, and keep going! Because it's really true; the better you feel, the faster you are heading towards what you want!"**

Pearl the Hawk flipped the coin back to Minty the Crocodile and said, "Take another look at our treasured golden coin. Now you will see The Golden Intention Code. If you read this morning and night you can check that you are taking your Navigator's advice and that you are on your way to reaching the desires you dream about."

"Er?" Minty the Crocodile was expecting to see the same words that he had seen just moments before. He looked down at their coin and then back up at his friends, stunned as he read the new mass of glowing words.

Golden Intention Code

Keep this golden coin from the end of the rainbow safe in your heart and soul for the rest of your life.

Here is The Golden Intention Code:

Everyone is special and I am too! When I feel great I'm heading for a life I'll love, so I look for the best in everything. I feel safe, relaxed, happy, loved and loving; loving myself and loving others. My dreams can come true and my life unfolds into a fantastic adventure!

I feel good about plenty of things in my life right now (think of a few)…and I feel great about what I see myself having…*(step into the movie screen in your mind and have fun dreaming of yourself enjoying your desires now).*

Play one of these Feel-Fab
Question and Answer Games by yourself or with your family.

In the Morning:

- What makes you smile, laugh and feel good? (think of different things)

- What's good about you? (pick different things)

- When will you have a relaxing moment today?

In the Evening:

- What was a good thing that happened today?

- What made you laugh today?

- What made you feel good about yourself today? (think of different things)

- What makes you feel most loved?

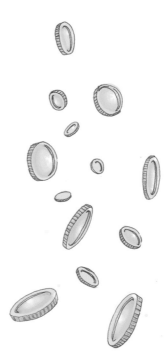

"How will all our wishes come true if we say The Golden Intention Code every night and morning and answer a few questions?" asked Clay the Badger.

"It's here, it says 'why' here. Let me read it!" growled Booster the Lion tapping the book with his paw. "It says…

> 'When you feel good saying each statement of The Golden Intention Code it means you are living by the code and you are confirming you agree with it. That means you are truly feeling good and heading for the things you want in life.
>
> But if you don't honestly feel really good when you read every line of the code, then you are heading away from what you want instead.
>
> To turn and head back in the right direction again remember the seven nuggets of advice on your golden coin. They will remind you of the upside of feeling good so that you start feeling better again… and when you are truly feeling good you are back on course and heading for the things you want'!"

Clay the Badger was still baffled "It's easy enough to read The Code before we go to sleep. But I still don't see how it means we'll have all our wishes, dreams and desires come true."

"Hold on, let me see." replied Booster the Lion looking back at the scrolls. "Ah yes, here we are…**The Golden Intention Code is like a code to unlock your inner brilliance! It makes absolutely certain that every bit of you feels good!"**

Pearl the Hawk sat up proudly and said cheerily to her friends, "Yes! Because then you are definitely following the guidance!"

"Ah ha!" exclaimed Chatty the Frog.

"But do we really need to do it every day?" asked Minty the Crocodile.

"No, but it certainly helps! Because then the code of intention becomes something that you live by. It means you get into the habit of always looking for ways to feel better throughout your day. It makes sure your life flows smoothly and you attract what you want. And the best time to do it is at night, just before you go to sleep and when you wake up."

"I was doing it! Yes! Yes! I think I was Surfing Rainbows at Diva's Jungle with my poorly eye!" shouted out Chatty the Frog. "I changed my mind and began to look at things differently. I began to feel hopeful and I began to feel better. I was Surfing Rainbows without even knowing it and my eye is healed!"

"Me too! Soon after I started to feel better about myself and my mane I fulfilled my dream of huge wealth!" exclaimed Booster the Lion.

"Yeah, yeah. And I reckon that's how I found my enormous collection of leaves!" said Sunny the Giraffe with a big grin on his face.

Pearl the Hawk looked at her excited friends and added, "Yup, we were all Surfing Rainbows."

Iris the Butterfly then added, "Stay feeling good about your dreams, even if others tell you that they're impossible. Remember that years ago it was considered impossible to walk on the moon, to have water running out of a tap, or to have light come on at a flick of a switch. Plenty have recovered from illnesses that were once considered incurable. What was once thought of as impossible is now commonplace! There's always a first time for everything."

Minty Meets a Friend

The group was thrilled about their discovery and they talked about it for quite a while longer.

Minty the Crocodile looked up mid-sentence, just as Sarah the Crocodile entered the room. Taken by surprise, his jaw dropped and he spilled the contents of his cup all over Booster the Lion! Quickly recovering from the shock of the hot sticky mess pouring down his chest, Booster pushed Minty's lower jaw up to close snugly with his top one and nudged him firmly out of his daze. Then Booster gave his friend a gentle shove off his chair. That was just as Sarah turned around. Minty quickly tried to regain his composure.

She had seen him. She was smiling! He hesitated. What if she didn't like him? Booster the Lion whispered a few encouraging words and pushed him forward.

Minty the Crocodile started to walk across the room to see his new friend in as relaxed and casual a manner as he could muster. His heart was racing. What would he say?

At last he reached her.

There was a deafening silence.

She smiled beautifully.

Minty the Crocodile stuttered, "Hi, you're pretty good at catching fish! That was a great move on the river bank the other day."

"Thanks, you did pretty well in the race too!" Sarah replied. Minty smiled happily. She was very friendly; what had he been worried about?

The rest of his friends back at the table watched as Minty and Sarah waggled their tails playfully at each other. She smiled and Minty grinned in return.

The Rainbow Surfers felt great to see their friend Minty so happy.

"Er. We're exploring further down the River of Life tomorrow," said Minty. "Would you like to come with us?"

"That sounds like fun," Sarah replied, still waggling her tail. "I'd love to!"

The End ...

In Sophia Rose's Study

It was still sunny outside when John and Maggie finished reading. As they turned over the last page Sophia Rose entered the study and asked her guests "Did you like it?"

Looking up John replied, "It seems that all we have to do is feel good!"

"Well yes," commented Sophia Rose smiling.

Maggie looked confused as she said, "Problem is...we're often made to do things that don't feel good! We don't have a choice!"

Sophia Rose sat down opposite them and said kindly, "Ah, but you do have a choice; you have the choice of where you set your point of view. And your point of view in life determines your direction and your destiny! When your point of view is always to look for the best in everything and you follow your good feelings, you are following your Navigator's guidance. As you look for ways of feeling better about everything that happens today, you improve what you attract to you tomorrow."

Both Maggie and John sat listening intently. They reckoned that since Surfing Rainbows had obviously worked so well for the famous singer it was definitely worth them giving it a go as well.

"If you want to attract the best in life," said Sophia, "Have fun dreaming up new desires and make them come alive on the movie screen in your mind! Dream about them as if you have them now! Even if they are things that you would like to have happen later that same day, in a few days, months or in the next few years. Step into your movie and benefit from all those good feelings! The great thing is that you don't need to work out how your desires will come about; all you have to do is follow your good feelings so that they can and will come about! It's like driving a car in a new town; you may not know the road ahead, but if you follow the signposts they will lead you to your destination.

Your good feelings will always be your guide. You may have the hunch to do something new, or be inspired to take one action or another, you may meet a person who will help you in some way, some things may happen as if by luck as with Booster the Lion at the waterfall. All sorts of things can happen that will help you achieve your dreams."

She paused and then said, "Just remember that when you start having bad feelings you start pushing your dreams out of your reach. So, if something happens in your day that makes you feel bad, decide how you would like the situation to turn out, and play that on the movie screen of your mind instead.

Be determined to always look for the best in everything, and take your mind off any worries by thinking about things that make you feel better. That's why it's so good to use The Golden Intention Code every day to make sure that you keep feeling really good... because the better you feel, the faster you'll be heading for your desires.

Then as you achieve this dream the never-ending cycle starts all over again as you dream about something new, which you either feel good or bad about, and so you either attract it to you quickly, slowly or not at all."

"It sounds so easy when you put it like that." said John "But we don't have your talent for singing. We don't have much talent for anything else either!"

"You may not sing like me, but I can't play soccer like you. I don't think of my singing in terms of talent but I love it when I sing. The more fun I've had the more successful I've become and the more I enjoy it.

Everyone is good at something. The more you enjoy what you're doing and the more you have fun doing it, the better you're likely to be at it, and soon you'll be following what you love doing, and that will inspire you with more dreams to reach for. Imagine yourself achieving those dreams on the movie in your mind too, and keep following your good feelings, because fulfilling any dream really is just made up of lots of little steps that feel good to you. Every step in the right direction will feel right, feel good, feel fun, and be inspiring! You just take one step at a time on your feel-good journey."

Sophia Rose smiled warmly as she continued, "That's what it means to go surfing rainbows!" As she finished, there was silence in the study for a moment or two while her visitors wondered about applying what she had just said to their own lives.

On the spur-of-the-moment Maggie jumped up and wrapped her arms around the famous singer, planting a warm kiss on her cheek. She was so grateful to their new friend for showing them how to go surfing rainbows. Sophia Rose was touched by Maggie's show of affection and was surprised when she saw the tears rolling down Maggie's cheeks.

Sophia Rose paused and then she said, "When I was very young I thought of it like this....the Rainbow Surfer characters represent the areas in life that affect our moods, and since the better we genuinely feel in all areas of our lives the faster we attract the desires we dream about, it's like the Rainbow Surfers live in each of us and when they are feeling good, so are we. That makes us what I call the HappyGoLuckeez, because the Rainbow Surfers feel magnificent and we lead happy, fulfilled lives.

Some people look at the world as a bad and miserable place, but you can choose to see all that's beautiful and magical instead. That's up to you. If you could fast forward to the end of your life and look in the mirror, do you want to be looking back at someone who has settled for a life of compromise or at someone who has enjoyed the very best that life has to offer?

Now it's your turn. You have the book. You can have so much fun Surfing Rainbows! Enjoy the films you make on the movie screen in your mind, follow your good feelings and turn your dreams into your reality. Let life's adventures really begin!"

"I'm going to start now," replied John.

Maggie nodded as she sat down beside her brother to take a closer look at The Golden Intention Code.

IF YOU DESIRE IT...
START SURFING RAINBOWS
FOR IT !!

Instructions for Cracking The Golden Intention Code:

1. In the morning and before going to sleep at night, pick a few different questions to enjoy from the following Table.

2. Then read the statements that make up The Golden Intention Code.

3. If any of The Code doesn't feel good to you when you read it go back through the Chapters of The Promise of Surfing Rainbows to find the golden coin with a nugget of advice for you. Look for the nugget of advice that is given in the same colour as the statement in the code that you feel bad about. This will remind you of the upside of feeling good.

4. Keep looking for ways to feel better and better so that when you reread The Golden Intention Code it feels great to you. That will mean you are back on track and heading for your dreams and desires again.

Golden Intention Code

Keep this golden coin from the end of the rainbow safe in your heart and soul for the rest of your life.

Here is The Golden Intention Code:

Everyone is special and I am too! When I feel great I'm heading for a life I'll love, so I look for the best in everything. I feel safe, relaxed, happy, loved and loving; loving myself and loving others. My dreams can come true and my life unfolds into a fantastic adventure!

I feel good about plenty of things in my life right now (think of a few)…and I feel great about what I see myself having…*(step into the movie screen in your mind and have fun dreaming of yourself enjoying your desires now)*.

Play one of these Feel-Fab
Question and Answer Games by yourself or with your family.

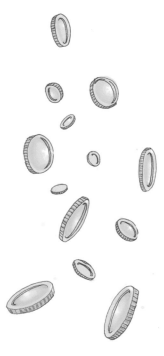

In the Morning:

- What makes you smile, laugh and feel good? (think of different things)

- What's good about you? (pick different things)

- When will you have a relaxing moment today?

In the Evening:

- What was a good thing that happened today?

- What made you laugh today?

- What made you feel good about yourself today? (think of different things)

- What makes you feel most loved?

Remember:

Throughout your day:

Whenever you ask yourself "What feels best?" you'll be safely making the best choice every time.

If something upsets you during your day, ask yourself this:

I want to feel better, so what's the best way I can look at this?

And what's the best thing that I would like to happen now?

(Imagine it happening – how does that feel?)

If someone upsets you during your day, remind yourself of this:

Despite what just happened, it is really worth looking for even the smallest thing about this person that you can feel is alright, so that it might help you begin to feel a little better. Take another moment; is there anything else that is okay about this person? Try to shift your mood. Next, take your mind off what has happened and think about other things that make you happy so that you head back on course to attracting better things to you instead.

When you relax:

When you would like some really good ideas to come to you, you can ask your Navigator a question…then see what comes to mind after you have relaxed for a while.

...and a
new beginning...

To see how Surfing Rainbows has helped many people achieve
their dreams please see www.SurfingRainbows.com

This is an interactive website and we would love to hear from
you too. Come and share your success Surfing Rainbows.

About the Authors

P. D. M. Dolce is a penname for the coauthors. These authors have experienced the power of Surfing Rainbows, as the technique came to be called, and have therefore seen their lives significantly changed for the better.

It was several years ago when two people who otherwise had nothing in common met on a bus and struck up a conversation. One was a young English woman who wanted nothing more than to start a family of her own. The other was a successful American businessman who was soon to become a grandfather for the second time. They were from very different worlds. They began a conversation that has lasted for over a decade and over thousands of miles. Their dialogue was about life, and the result is The Promise of Surfing Rainbows. Both of them had read all the self-help books they could lay their hands on. As they shared information with each other, it became clear to them that as wonderful and helpful as those books had been, there might be something missing. They set about finding what that "something" could be and that was the gist of their transatlantic phone conversations over the years. After much discussion, trial and error, more reading, and more experiments, they pinpointed what is now being called, The Crucial Link. Once that happened and they applied the information to their lives, everything changed for them.

We know without a doubt the information contained in this book works because you are holding in your hands absolute proof that it does. You see, there is a key, a crucial link, that allows you to get whatever you want or desire in life deliberately, by design, and not by happenstance. And the book you are reading right now is the direct result of the authors applying Surfing Rainbows.

Our desire is the same for you. We want you to know how to Rainbow Surf too. Picture your life as a treasure hunt for unlimited treasures because life should be fun and exciting. And it can be!

Let the good times flow.

This is the promise of Surfing Rainbows.

The Promise of Surfing Rainbows Storybook

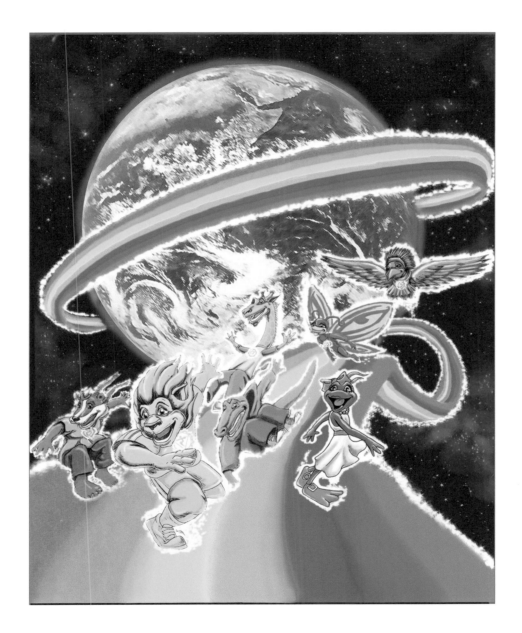

Please visit our interactive website at www.SurfingRainbows.com for more information on other great Rainbow Surfing ideas, events, contact information and more.

Printed in the United States
By Bookmasters